Murder on the Marginal Way

A Michael Bishop Mystery

D1522619

by

Anthony J. Pucci

This book is a work of fiction. Names, characters, places, and incidents are a product of the author's imagination or are used fictitiously. Any resemblance to actual events, locales, or persons, living or dead, is coincidental.

Epigraph

"Il n'y a pas de secrets que le temps ne révèle pas."

"There are no secrets that time does not reveal."

Jean-Baptiste Racine

Chapter One

He pulled off his tee shirt, dropped it on the sand, kicked off his sandals, and sprinted toward the water. Unfazed by the initial contact with the frigid ocean temperature, he dove into a cresting breaker, and a moment later, bobbed up for air. The morning sun caught the droplets as he shook the excess water from his hair.

He focused on the beach where a beautiful dark-haired woman stood with her arms folded against the stiff ocean breeze. "Come on in," he shouted. "The water's perfect."

Grace backed farther away from the water's edge at the very thought. She shouted over the pounding surf, "Are you out of your mind, Michael Bishop? I'm freeeezing!"

He motioned for her to join him, but she just laughed and shook her head back and forth. Even though the morning sun glimmered brightly on the water, a storm churning at sea brought a series of high swells. Michael bobbed up and down as he let several waves pass him. When he saw the one he wanted, he waited until just the right moment to launch himself, arms together and fully extended. He rode that thunderous wave all the way in until his stomach grazed the muddy sand.

Shivering and dripping wet, he ran toward her as she applauded, either in recognition of his skill in body surfing or in appreciation that he had come out of the water. He opened his arms to embrace her, but she shied away.

"Here," she said as she tossed him a thick beach towel, "you need to dry off first."

He swung the towel around his shoulders and wiped his face and hair. He looked into the sparkling eyes of his bride of three days, extended the towel like a cape, and drew her to him. As they embraced, he knew that he was the luckiest man alive.

***

They were staying at a small waterfront cottage on Lilac Street about a quarter of a mile from the center of Ogunquit, Maine. Grace's grandparents, Carmine and Rosa Ippolito, had given the use of the cottage as their wedding gift to the young couple who could not have afforded the ninety dollars per week rental fee. At low tide, they took long walks on the beach; at high tide, they walked the Marginal Way, a one-and-a-quarter-mile stretch of the one of the most stunning coastal paths on the entire Atlantic. Grace was allergic to fish, but that didn't stop Michael from feasting on lobster, seafood chowder, calamari, scallops, and steamers, none of which cost more than three dollars and fifty cents. At night, they made love listening to the soothing sounds of the tides.

In a couple of weeks, he would begin teaching English at Holy Trinity High School in Groveland, a small town in upstate New York. He thought that he might stay there a few years, gain some experience, work on his doctorate, and eventually become a college professor. He also thought that he would enjoy his golden years with Grace by his side. As it turned out, he was wrong on both counts.

***

Each summer, Michael and Grace returned to Ogunquit which means "beautiful place by the sea" in the language of the Native American Abenaki tribe. Michael agreed that it was indeed a beautiful place, although he would have preferred to vacation elsewhere on occasion. For Grace, however, it was a chance to visit family and the place where she spent her childhood summers. After her grandparents passed away, it had become so much of a tradition that they continued to make their way there even as the summer population grew larger, and the rentals grew outrageously more expensive. For a precious couple of weeks, they could forget all of their worries and simply enjoy the sea, the sun, the sand, and each other.

That all ended when Grace unexpectedly died of a ruptured appendix. They had been married for thirty-eight years. Michael, struggling with his loss, chose to stay home that summer and the summers since then. Ogunquit was associated in his mind with so many fond memories of their times together that he could not imagine going there alone. His thinking did not change until almost ten years later.

***

It was only last night that he had decided that a week in Ogunquit might provide just the rejuvenation of spirit that he needed before beginning his forty-seventh year teaching English at Holy Trinity High School. He packed enough clothes for his stay as well as plenty of food, treats, and toys for Max, the Jack Russell terrier that had become an important part of his life within the last year or so. Luckily, Max traveled well, although frequent stops were necessary as much for Bishop as for the dog. It was early Sunday evening when he crossed the bridge over the Piscataqua River into the state of Maine. In a few short minutes, he pulled into the parking lot of the Belvedere Inn, relieved to see a "Vacancy" sign swaying gently in the ocean breeze.

Bishop put a leash on Max who bounded out of the car, unable to contain his desire to explore his new surroundings. After sitting in his Toyota Corolla for most of the day, Bishop also felt a surge of excitement as he once again returned to this special town. However, he also felt his age as he walked somewhat stiffly into the spacious lobby and up to the front desk.

"Mr. Bishop, what a surprise!"

He was very accustomed to bumping into former students in and around his small hometown of Groveland, but he was more than four hundred miles away. In the last few years, he had begun to experience some memory issues. As he looked at the woman who greeted him, he hoped that he would be able to match the face with a name. Bishop guessed her to be in her early thirties. Of medium height and slender build, she had straight dark hair parted off to one side and large brown eyes that lit up when she smiled.

"Amy Walsh! You look just the same as you did when you graduated from high school. How nice to see you!" He held Max's leash tightly in his left hand as he reached out to shake hands with his former student. She leaned over the counter to give him a hug. Max jumped up expecting a treat or at least some attention.

"The years have been kind to you as well," she said. Whether she really meant that or was just being polite, Bishop accepted the compliment. "How long have you been retired?"

"Actually, I haven't retired yet. I still enjoy teaching."

"Wow! Good for you!"

Unexpectedly bumping into former students sometimes created other problems for him even if he remembered the name. There were occasions when that was all he could remember about a student who had been in his classroom for an entire school year. Considering the number of students that he had encountered during his career, perhaps he could be forgiven if he didn't remember any specifics, but it still bothered him. Often, students would share some of their vivid memories of what he had said or done. Others mentioned certain works of literature that they still remembered.

Amy was one that he recalled clearly. Not only had she been in his Advanced Placement English class in her senior year, she also had served as the editor-in-chief of *The Beacon*, the school newspaper that Bishop moderated. She was a beautiful girl then, and she was a beautiful young woman now. As he recalled, she had been voted by her senior classmates as the May Queen, the girl who best embodied the Christian values of the Virgin Mary. Much had happened since she graduated in what Bishop figured to be the early 2000s, and he was hoping to have a chance to chat with her for a bit.

Just then the phone rang. Since she was the only person working the desk at the moment, she excused herself to take the call. When Bishop realized that the caller was not inquiring about reservations, he admired some of the large aerial photos of the area that hung on the walls as he walked Max around the lobby.

"David, I told you that that was your last chance. Do you understand me?" Amy's tone had changed markedly as she spoke with this man. It was impossible for Bishop not to hear every word of her side of the conversation. She listened for a moment as David said something.

"Don't bother. I'll mail you your paycheck first thing tomorrow." She paused again, and Bishop caught a glimpse of the frustration that was written across her face. "No! And please don't call again!" With that she placed the phone back on the receiver.

As Bishop returned to the desk, she apologized for the interruption but made no attempt to explain what it was all about. Of course, it was none of his business, so he did not ask even though he was curious as to what would cause her to become so upset.

"How can I help you, Mr. Bishop?" That beautiful smile and gentle demeanor had returned.

"My late wife and I used to vacation in Ogunquit every year, but we never stayed at the Belvedere. It's such a gem. I'd like to book a single room for a week," he announced. Before he could reach for his credit card, she shook her head in regret.

"Oh, dear! I'm afraid I can't help you." She looked down at Max. "We don't allow pets regardless of how cute they are."

The disappointment on his face was palpable. "I was afraid that might happen."

Amy had a bit more bad news. "And dogs aren't allowed on the beach or on the Marginal Way. There's a hundred dollar fine," she added.

"Did you hear that Max?" he asked his companion facetiously. "I guess a lot has changed since I was last here."

"I'm so sorry," Amy said sincerely.

"It's certainly not your fault. I didn't do my homework," he said with a grin on his face.

A young couple with a child of about three entered the lobby as Bishop prepared to leave. The little boy scampered toward Max. "Doggie!" he said excitedly as he pointed at his target.

"Alex, no! Come here, please," his mother said firmly.

Bishop quickly dropped to his knees to intercept the excited child who paid no attention to his mother. He caught him in his arms, lifted him up in the air, and handed him gently to the concerned mom. "Max won't bite, but he does tend to jump a lot, and I didn't want him to knock over the little guy."

With a look of relief on her face, she thanked Bishop as she cradled the little one in her arms. Knowing that Amy would be busy dealing with the needs of this family and those of an older couple just entering, Bishop led Max toward the exit. It was getting late anyway, and he needed to find a place to stay.

"It was wonderful to see you, Amy. Perhaps I'll stop by later in the week just to catch up."

"If you don't mind waiting a few minutes, Mr. Bishop, I may be able to help you," Amy said warmly.

"Take your time,' replied her former teacher. He didn't know what she had in mind since it was obvious that she couldn't override the no-pets rule, but there was no harm in waiting. He took Max out for a walk around the building. Bishop admired the meticulously kept flower gardens as Max sniffed the ocean air and tried to chase a monarch butterfly.

After Amy had registered the two parties, Bishop approached the desk again. Amy picked up the phone and began punching in some numbers. Before she finished, she explained, "I'm calling Martha Littleford. Her ancestors once owned about half of the town. She's in real estate now. We don't always get along, but I think she's looking for a couple of weekly renters."

Bishop hoped for the best as he heard one side of the conversation.

"Martha, it's Amy at the Belvedere. How are you?"

Amy's hopeful expression quickly changed to one of frustration. "I know you're upset, but what's done is done, right?" Before giving the woman a chance to respond, she launched into her reason for calling. "Anyway, one of my old teachers from high school just walked in here out of the blue. He's looking for a room for a week, but he has a dog. Do you have anything for him?" She held up her left hand with fingers crossed as she waited for a reply. Several bracelets slid a few inches from her wrist.

Bishop was grateful for Amy's help, but if she and Martha were on the outs, he worried about what "anything" might turn out to be. He was also mildly surprised that Amy referred to him as her

12

"old" teacher instead of "former" teacher. Maybe she meant what she said. He was over seventy years old.

After listening for a moment, she said, "I realize weeklies start on a Saturday. Just see what you've got, please," she added as she glanced at Bishop and rolled her eyes. After another pause, she picked up a pen and began jotting down some information.

"Uh huh… Uh huh … got it! Thanks, Mart! You're a peach … yeah, I'll send him right over."

As she wiped her brow in mock relief and ripped a sheet from a pad of paper, Amy flashed a big smile. "She's really more of a peach pit, but anyway, she's got something I think you're gonna like. The party that was supposed to be there cancelled at the last minute so they forfeited their payment. "

Bishop beamed as gleefully as if he had won the lottery. Inwardly, he was worried about how much this "something" was going to cost. If he declined, he would come off as ungrateful. On the other hand, since he had taken this trip without checking availability and prices, he knew he should feel grateful for Amy's help in finding a place to stay. In addition, Max was becoming increasingly agitated as his dinnertime approached.

Amy handed over the slip of paper, as she explained, "It's an adorable two-bedroom cottage with all the amenities of home on Israel Head Road, and the ocean view is spectacular. I'd kill to buy one of those cottages. You can easily access the Marginal Way from there …" She paused for a moment, leaned over the counter to look at Max, and continued, " … minus Max, of course."

"Luckily, he sleeps a lot during the day," he said as he reached down to give the older dog some attention. Taking a quick glance at the paper he had been handed, he saw the dates of his stay, the street address of the cottage, and the contact name of the agent. What he didn't see was the rental fee. What if it were outrageously high?

"This place sounds perfect, Amy, but I'm a bit worried about the expense. Did Ms. Littleford happen to mention the rate?"

She seemed a bit embarrassed that she hadn't checked with him on that before she ended the call. "Oh, my gosh! I'm so sorry! I guess I wasn't thinking. She's asking fifteen hundred for the rest of the week plus tax. Is that okay?" She cringed a bit not knowing how her former teacher would respond. She added more to herself than to Bishop, "That devil already pocketed two thousand from the cancellation."

Bishop did some quick math in his head. It was definitely more per night than he had expected to pay, but he could economize by avoiding expensive restaurants. It probably wasn't much more per night than he would have spent at the Belvedere anyway.

"I can manage that," he said with a smile. "It's not as if I'm jetting all over the globe." He didn't tell Amy that it was the first real vacation he had taken since his wife passed away almost ten years ago. "Thanks so much for all of your help," he said as he reached out to shake her hand.

"My pleasure!" she replied. "You were one of my favorite teachers at Trinity. Perhaps we can grab a coffee during the week. It would be fun to talk over old times."

"That sounds like a plan. Do you work this desk most days?"

"Actually, no. I'm filling in for someone that failed to show for work. Most of the time, I'm in my office. I'm the manager here," she said proudly.

"Really? Congratulations! I'm glad that you've done so well."

"Thank you."

"I best be on my way."

"Just take a right when you get to the end of our driveway. Littleford Realty will be on your right about a half a mile down. Ask for Kelli Dempsey. She'll take care of you."

"Not Martha?"

"No, she's too old and cranky to deal very much with the public. I'm sure she spends most of her time trying to figure out how she can stab someone in the back."

Bishop just raised his eyebrows at that remark. He thanked Amy again and said that he was looking forward to getting together with her sometime during the week.

As he and Max walked back to his car, he had no idea that his anticipated meeting with his former student would never take place.

Chapter Two

At about the same time that Bishop was finalizing arrangements for his stay with Kelli at the realtor's office, Ron Jennings received a phone call from Sister Estelle Molloy, Superior General of the Sisters of the Holy Rosary, the order of nuns that sponsored Holy Trinity High School. Bishop considered Ron, one of the assistant principals, his closest friend on the staff. For the last few months, he had been serving as the interim principal after Sister Estelle delivered a personnel bombshell.

Sister Ann Cowie had been relieved of her duties as principal, and her close friend and co-conspirator in numerous misadventures, Sister Pat Meehan was similarly dispatched from her position as an assistant principal. The Superior General had taken this decisive action in part as the result of some undercover work done by her assistant, Blake Driscoll. The last weeks of the school year had played out uneventfully with Ron at the helm. He took to his new role quite well, and the mere absence of Sisters Ann and Pat, often referred to as Mayhem and Meany, had brightened the mood of staff and students alike. Since Ron had applied for appointment as the principal for the new school year, he was expecting that call from Sister Estelle. What he hadn't anticipated was what she had to say.

***

After his brief conversation with Sister Estelle, Ron's first call was to Mary Ellen Webster to whom he had recently become engaged. She had served as the business manager at Trinity until she ran afoul of the two sisters after a short time on the job. She resigned rather than give them the pleasure of firing her. From that brief experience and from Ron's stories about some of their more outrageous exploits, she wasn't terribly surprised by the news. She was, however, furious and urged Ron to resign immediately. Ron expected such a fiery outburst from her. Once she had a chance to think a situation through, she usually saw things differently. His second call was to his good friend and confidant, Michael Bishop.

When Bishop pulled into the driveway of 89 Israel Head Road, he was less inclined to grumble about the cost. From the outside, the place was absolutely perfect. The first floor featured a large enclosed porch, and the front room on the second floor had sliding glass doors leading to a deck over the porch that would provide a tremendous view of the rocky coast. Inside, the place was tastefully furnished and in immaculate condition. As he imagined, the front room upstairs was the master bedroom with its own full bath. How could he complain about the price? Considering the facts that he hadn't done any planning for the trip and that many places do not allow pets, he had been quite fortunate to bump into Amy.

The enclosed porch was the ideal spot for Max. After getting him settled, Bishop grabbed his house key and was about to walk the short distance into the center of town to find a place for dinner when his cell rang. When Ron's name popped up on the screen, he assumed that his friend was just checking that he had arrived safely. Although that might have been part of the reason for the call, it was by no means the only reason.

"Hope I didn't catch you at a bad time," Ron said.

Bishop was tired and hungry after his drive of over four hundred miles, but he replied, "Not at all. Is everything all right?"

"I just took a call from Sister Estelle," he said flatly.

Bishop knew from his tone of voice that the news hadn't been good. He had written a strong letter of recommendation for his friend, and now Bishop feared that his support might have actually worked against Ron.

"Well, what did she have to say?" He involuntarily held his breath as he waited for an answer.

"I didn't get the job," Ron said. His disappointment was obvious.

"I'm so sorry! Did she explain why?"

"Since I was doing such an outstanding job as the assistant principal for discipline, she felt that it was beneficial to the school that I remain in that capacity."

"Very clever on her part. Compliment you while simultaneously giving you bad news. If you are doing such a great job in her eyes, you should have asked her for a raise," Bishop added, trying to lighten the mood, although he knew that the likelihood of her granting that request was nil.

Clearly his attempt failed as Ron made no response.

"Did you ask her who would be taking over as the principal?"

"I certainly did. I mean I didn't even know who the other candidates were let alone who was given the job or why."

Bishop was gripped by curiosity. In his forty-plus years at Trinity, he had worked under three principals, each with their own strengths and weaknesses. He hoped that whoever had been selected would have more of the former and less of the latter.

"Well, is it someone we know or someone from out of town?"

Ron laughed mysteriously as he answered, "Both!"

"That doesn't make any sense."

"Yes, it does," insisted Jennings without offering an explanation. He sometimes frustrated Bishop with his ability to answer a question without really providing an answer.

Bishop had been convinced that Ron would get the job. Since the whole hiring process had been kept under wraps by Sister Estelle and Trinity's board, he couldn't even hazard a guess. Whoever it was had to be an improvement over the disgraced Sister Ann.

"Okay, Ron, I have no clue. Who is the new principal?"

"The old principal," he said cryptically.

Bishop was getting on in years himself. He wasn't sure that selecting an older person was the right approach, but at least whoever it was had years of experience.

"How old?"

"Mike, I'm not talking about age. I hope you're ready for this because I certainly wasn't. The new principal is the old principal, the Mayhem of Mayhem and Meany, Sister Ann Cowie."

***

Bishop was stunned. Sister Ann … returning to Holy Trinity … as principal? A few months earlier, Bishop had thought that he might never see her again. Along with her cohort, the rotund Sister Pat, she had been suspended indefinitely for her countless examples of poor judgment, poor communication, and poor leadership to say nothing of a series of indiscretions that were morally bankrupt if not criminal. Sister Estelle had sent her to work in a home for battered women. How had she managed to wrangle her way back?

"Mike, are you there?"

Ron's question shook him from his reverie. "Yes, I'm here. I'm so sorry, Ron. Everyone thought you did an outstanding job as interim principal. I just can't believe this. It is so wrong on so many levels."

"You won't get an argument from me," he said with a hint of a laugh that belied his disappointment and frustration.

Bishop sat down at the circular oak dining room table and put his keys down. He noticed some blue jays perched on a power line above a tall hedge of lilacs that marked the boundary of the small backyard. Their squawks pierced the air as they suddenly took flight. Had they also heard the disturbing news? Unlike them, he couldn't fly away, nor did he want to. Her return was an affront to common sense, and he was determined to get some answers.

"Did you ask Sister Estelle to explain her decision in allowing that woman to return?"

"Of course I did."

"How could she possibly justify her change of heart? Wasn't Blake's scathing indictment of Sister Ann enough to warrant a permanent change in leadership?"

"She didn't mention Blake or his report at all. She did say that she consulted with the board. Apparently, they had concerns about my lack of experience as a principal although they appreciated how well I had 'held the fort' after the suspensions."

"That doesn't make any sense. You proved that you could handle the job, and they admitted it. I'm going to have some questions for Art Gleason when I get back. He's still the board chairman, isn't he?"

"Yes, he is, as far as I know, but please don't intervene on my behalf," Ron urged. "It won't accomplish anything."

"It will satisfy my curiosity," countered Bishop.

"I'd really prefer that you don't pursue it."

Bishop realized that he had to respect his friend's request. "Okay, but what else did Sister Estelle say?"

"She kept saying that Sister Ann was very contrite about her past behavior and asked for a second chance."

"Second chance?" Bishop said incredulously. "How many second chances did she give to so many people over the years? Did she give Mary Ellen a second chance?" Through no fault of her own, Mary Ellen's first payroll as business manager was botched. With prodding from Sister Pat, the principal brought down the ax.

"Believe me," said Ron sadly, "that was my first thought. She also reminded me that it is a special charism of the Sisters of the Holy Rosary to show mercy and compassion."

"How often did Mayhem and Meany show mercy and compassion?" he asked rhetorically. Bishop knew how difficult a conversation that must have been. There was nothing that he could say to soften the blow, but there was something that he could do. Each year, he gave some thought to retiring. Now that Sister Ann was once again the principal, there was no way that he would consider retiring for the foreseeable future. Sister Ann might have convinced Sister Estelle that she was deserving of a second chance, but Bishop suspected that it wouldn't take long for the principal to fall back into her old ways.

"What about Sister Pat?" asked Bishop. She had been sent to work in a soup kitchen as she considered the future of her vocation.

"Estelle didn't mention her, and I didn't ask," Ron stated simply.

"Without Pat to muddy the waters, Ann might be able to do a decent job. We'll have to give her the benefit of the doubt."

"I know."

"When is she arriving?"

"Tomorrow. Sister Estelle said that the faculty, staff, and parents would receive an email in the morning announcing the decision. I'll tell you something, Mike. As the only administrator available, I haven't taken one day of vacation this summer. I don't think I want to be here for the first day of her return."

"I don't blame you at all. You need some time off." After a moment's pause, he asked, "Why don't you come up here for a few days? I've just rented a two-bedroom, two-bathroom cottage on the waterfront."

Without any hesitation, Ron perked up. "Seriously? That sounds very tempting."

"There's only one problem," Bishop said in mock seriousness.

"What's that?"

"You have to share your bedroom with Max."

They both laughed as Ron accepted his friend's offer. A few quiet days at the beach was just the medicine that he needed. Neither man had any idea that the next week would be anything but relaxing.

Chapter Three

After he made sure that Max was settled in his new surroundings, Bishop picked up his house key, put on a hat and a windbreaker, and started walking toward Shore Road. Early evenings in late August in this part of the country tend to be chilly, and he thought the walk would help him work the kinks out after a long drive. He headed for Bessie's Restaurant on Main Street.

As he approached the downtown area, he was glad that he had decided to walk. It had been a beautiful day and throngs of tourists still gravitated to this special beach town, determined to enjoy every last bit of summer. The restaurant was located at the intersection of Shore Road, Main Street, and Beach Street. Minus any streetlights, the cars edged along at a pace no faster than what he could achieve by walking, and it was clear that he would have been frustrated in his search for a parking place.

When he walked into Bessie's, he hung up his light jacket and placed his hat on the shelf above the coat rack. A young woman with dark hair pulled back in a ponytail smiled and greeted him with her heavy accent.

"Gud eveninck, sir. Wan for deener?"

He returned her smile and nodded in agreement.

She scanned the dining area and turned back to him. "I only have booth. Is okay?" Despite some obvious difficulties with the language, she spoke quite rapidly. He would have to pay close attention when she spoke. Again, he nodded.

"Pleese, follow me," she said as she led him to his seat. She was wearing a t-shirt promoting Bessie's, a pair of skinny jeans, and sneakers. After he situated himself in the booth, she put a paper placemat and silverware on the table and handed him a menu.

"My name is Orjana. I'll be bak in a minutes to take your order," she announced before setting off on her next task.

After studying the menu for a few moments, he placed his order for a turkey club sandwich and hot tea. As he waited for Orjana to return, his thoughts drifted back to his conversation with Ron. It seemed to him a travesty that Sister Ann had been given an opportunity to return as the principal. One question kept bothering him like an itch that he couldn't scratch. What was the real reason that Sister Estelle reversed her initial decision?

Of course it was possible that Sister Ann with her poker face had convinced her superior that she had truly changed. Knowing the principal for as many years as he had, he found it implausible that such a conversion had taken place. It was far more likely that the wily nun had some knowledge, some secret, that she used as leverage to make her triumphant return to Holy Trinity. He couldn't blame Ron for wanting to be elsewhere for that.

Orjana brought him his dinner. The sandwich was enormous, and the plate overflowed with rippled potato chips. "Pleese enjoy. I will chain you to seet unteel you eet every bite," she added with a straight face.

His curiosity got the best of him, and he asked, "Are you from Slovenia?"

"My God, yes! Most people guess Russia. How did you know dat?"

"I'm really not sure," he said with a laugh. He wondered how a young woman from Slovenia ended up in Ogunquit, Maine. If he had a chance during the week, perhaps he would find out.

As he ate his sandwich that tasted even better than it looked, he returned to Sister Estelle's decision. Perhaps there was nothing nefarious in it. He recalled the words of Portia, disguised as a wise young lawyer, speaking to Shylock on the nature of mercy in William Shakespeare's *The Merchant of Venice.* "It is enthroned in the heart of kings,/ It is an attribute to God himself;/ And earthly power doth then show likest God's/ When mercy seasons justice."

Had Estelle taken the God-like path in her handling of the case, or had she been duped by a member of her own order? Time would tell, and with school starting in a matter of days, he would have his answer soon enough.

He finished his sandwich, teased Orjana that she wouldn't have to chain him to his seat, and declined dessert although he had seen a number of tempting pies and cakes in a glass case as he walked in. He left a generous tip, and as he left the restaurant, she called to him, "Tank you, and I hope you weel come bak."

"Yes, I'm planning on it." He grabbed his windbreaker and walked back to his cottage on Israel Head Road to find Max asleep on the oval braid rug in the porch. It had been a long day for him as well.

***

The fog was so thick the next morning that he couldn't see the water from the deck outside of his bedroom. After feeding Max, he grabbed his light jacket that was draped over a chair in the kitchen where he had left it the night before. However, he couldn't find his hat. He checked the foyer closet. Empty. He went back upstairs and checked the bedroom. No hat. He was almost certain that he had it when he went to Bessie's.

Over the last couple of years, he had become somewhat forgetful which was a source of some concern. He hoped that it was just a normal part of aging and nothing more. It hadn't affected his ability to teach, but it was annoying and sometimes embarrassing. Convincing himself that he had simply misplaced the hat, he took Max out for a walk. It was a chance for Bishop to explore the neighborhood. He had been fortunate to rent that cottage. Of course, Amy had been a big part of that, and he would repay her kindness by picking up the check when they met for lunch.

Max's wet nose soon became coated in beach sand as he stopped to sniff as often as he could. Bishop wanted him to get a good walk in this morning since he would be house bound for a good part of the day. They walked down Cherry Lane, one of the access points to the Marginal Way. The fog was beginning to burn off, and he could hear the waves slapping at the jagged rocks. Since dogs weren't allowed on that path, he walked the roads nearby. He passed one impressive home after another. He wondered which one Grace, who had been a realtor for many years, would have picked as her favorite. The only people he saw out this early were professional

27

landscapers cleaning flower beds, trimming hedges or mowing lawns.

After letting Max back into the cottage, he had two items on his immediate agenda. He needed to get something for breakfast, and since the fridge contained only ice cubes, he needed to do some grocery shopping. It took just a few moments to get on Route 1 where morning traffic bogged down. This old road actually spanned from Maine to Florida. He and his wife often said that they would make that trip one day. That never happened.

Heading north toward Wells, he pulled into a Dunkin' Donuts. He sat down at a booth and enjoyed a Boston cream doughnut and a cup of green tea … not the most nutritious breakfast, but he was on vacation, he reasoned. Farther up the road, he pulled into the mostly empty parking lot of a Hannaford's supermarket. Vacation or not, he couldn't avoid food shopping, a chore that he dreaded.

He grabbed a large cart and went up and down the aisles, tossing in all of the staples as he saw them. He had noticed a gas grill in the backyard of the cottage, and he planned to make good use of that. Ron would be arriving late in the afternoon, and although Bishop knew that he hated preparing meals as much as he did, they couldn't eat all of their meals out. As he headed to the checkout counter, he was convinced of two things. First, no matter how attentive he had been, he probably forgot a basic item that would necessitate another trip to the store. Second, given Ron's appetite, it was unlikely that he would be throwing anything away at the end of the week.

As he placed all of the plastic bags in the trunk of his car, he heard someone approach.

"Hey, mister!"

Bishop turned around to see one of the store clerks running toward him holding a bag of groceries. He was a solidly built tall man with red hair and several tattoos on his arms. "You forgot this," he said as he handed over the bag.

Glancing at the name tag pinned to his shirt, Bishop said, "Thank you very much, Kiki. I'm afraid it's not the first time I've done that." He had the vague feeling that he knew this man, but obviously the man, probably in his mid-twenties, did not know him. The veteran teacher concluded that he resembled one of his former students although he couldn't come up with a name.

"No problem, sir. Have a nice day."

"The same to you," and gesturing to the bag that he had left in the store, he added, "and thanks again."

Despite Kiki's parting words, Bishop's day turned out to be anything but nice.

***

After putting away the groceries and unpacking the rest of his clothes, he went into the porch and opened all the windows. He sat down in the thickly cushioned chaise as Max settled down on the rug. It seemed the perfect time to relax with some classical music in the background, but his extensive CD collection remained at home.

The sounds of the incoming tide, however, more than compensated for that. Within moments, he was sound asleep.

The pinging sound of his cell phone startled him awake about an hour later. The text from Ron indicated that he was running late and that he didn't expect to arrive until 7 or so in the evening. He texted back that they would have dinner when he arrived. It took Bishop a few minutes to fully wake up from his unplanned nap.

"Max, how about a long walk before lunch?"

Apparently, "walk" was the only word other than his name that Max understood, as he scampered to the door where his owner slipped on his leash. Bishop didn't need his windbreaker at this hour of the day, but he could have used his hat to protect himself from the sun's rays, still strong at this time of the year. It irked him that he hadn't found the hat that was a rather expensive Tilley. Perhaps he had left it at the restaurant the previous night. When he first purchased the UV-protected, water-repellent hat, he had printed his initials on the underside of the back brim but neglected to register his purchase with the company. Guaranteed for life against wear, it wasn't guaranteed against the forgetfulness of the owner. He called Bessie's to see if someone had turned it in, but no one knew anything about it. Was it possible that he had it this morning and left it at the Dunkin' Donuts or at Hannaford's? In either case, finding it now was probably a lost cause. He would buy a cheap beach hat to get him through the rest of the week.

***

With the news of Sister Ann's return to Holy Trinity, he had a lot to think about as he headed toward Perkins Cove which was the site of number of old fishing shacks that had been converted to artisans' studios, gift shops, and restaurants. Instead of walking the Marginal Way to get there, because of Max, he stayed on the town roads. He bought himself a lemonade, sat at a bench near the entrance (or exit) to the popular walking path, admiring the views of the draw bridge over the Ogunquit River leading out to sea. He gave Max most of the ice from his drink.

All in all, his first day at the beach had gone fairly well. Suddenly, everything went wrong. He had hooked Max's leash over the handle on the side of the bench, but Max managed to get loose. He headed straight for the Marginal Way and a hundred dollar fine for his owner.

"Max! Max! Come here, boy!" His shouts were fruitless as the dog never even looked back. Perhaps he had seen something that he felt the urge to chase. Perhaps he just needed to run. In any event, Bishop began to run after him, pleading with him to stop, bribing him with the promise of a treat. The site of a dog running along the path and this older man chasing him startled some of the many people walking the path. Bishop had to weave his way around some slow walkers that he approached from behind as he kept his eye on other walkers moving toward him. Max was now well ahead of him, and Bishop was breathing harder as he navigated the rather narrow path and its slight incline.

Just as he was about out of gas, a younger man sprinted by him, saying, "Don't worry. I'll get your dog."

With another sharp turn in the path, he lost sight of both the man and the dog. He was breathing heavily and sweating freely when he approached a short wooden bridge on the path. The young man, shirtless and wearing a bandana, had managed to grab the leash that had trailed Max the whole time.

The man turned around to hand the leash to the dog's owner.

"Kiki!" he said in total surprise. This was the polite young man who had run out to the parking lot at Hannaford's with a bag of groceries that he had left behind. "Man, am I glad to see you! I never would have caught up with him." Max was behaving oddly. He kept barking and jumping around, and would have tried to scamper down to the slippery rocks and the water below if he wasn't restrained.

"This is the second time today that you've come to my rescue," said a grateful Bishop.

"No problem, sir. I just happened to see the dog take off and thought I could run faster than you." Bishop laughed at the understatement as he introduced himself and shook Kiki's hand.

"You better get him off the path before you get hit with a hundred dollar fine," he advised. Some of the walkers from both directions slowed down to see what was going on. Max wouldn't stop barking.

"Max, what is the matter with you?" Bishop was frustrated and embarrassed. The dog had never acted this way before. He turned to Kiki. "Would you hold onto him for a moment, please?"

Kiki got down on his haunches, held on to Max's collar with one hand, and patted him with the other. With Max restrained, Bishop carefully took a few steps down the sandy slope toward the rocks below. What could Max be so interested in? As he inched farther down, the water swirling among the rocks seemed more menacing. Several seagulls swooped overhead. There was a long crevice in the rock formation, and he craned his neck to look down into it.

The blood drained from his face, but it wasn't from fear of falling. Wedged into the crevice was the body of Amy Walsh.

Chapter Four

"Call 911!" he managed to shout.

As if the unexpected discovery wasn't enough of a jolt, the fact that he knew the victim intensified his grief. Although there were tide pools nearby, Amy's body was not submerged. She was wearing a tank top, running shorts, and sneakers. Bishop noticed a gash on her forehead and several abrasions on her torso, undoubtedly caused as she tumbled against the rocks. She must have been listening to music as she jogged since he could see the earbuds that had been dislodged as she fell.

He knew that the image of her lying there with her eyes staring blankly would be one that he would never forget. He desperately wanted to close those eyes, but he knew that he could not possibly reach her. In the past, he had walked the Marginal Way many times, and he knew that some places had protective fencing, but large expanses did not. He also had noticed as he chased after Max that the path, although mostly paved, was anything but smooth. Obviously, she had been jogging, and she must have tripped or lost her balance. It was such a senseless tragedy.

Slowly and carefully, he made his way back to the safety of the path. Several passersby gathered to find out what had happened. One elderly couple near him spoke to each other in hushed tones as others strained to get a glimpse of the unfolding tragedy.

"Help is on the way," Kiki informed him as he led Bishop to one of the benches that lined the path. "I think that you ought to sit down for a moment."

Bishop nodded his agreement as he hugged Max for comfort. He was still somewhat dazed as he heard the sirens of an emergency response vehicle. Because of the narrowness of the path, a team arrived on foot carrying their rescue equipment. However much he might have hoped for a different outcome, he knew there would be no rescue. They would have to rappel Amy's body to the level of the path and then carry her to the waiting ambulance.

As the recovery process began, more people stopped to watch. Several officers arrived on the scene, and one of them kept the crowd at a distance. Another officer was asking around to see if there had been any witnesses. The elderly couple looked around and pointed to Bishop who was still seated on the bench.

As the officer approached, Bishop stood, holding Max's leash tightly. He was a stocky man in his mid-thirties wearing the grey uniform of the Ogunquit Police Department.

"My name is Officer Ben Minnehan, sir. Did you witness this?" he asked as he gestured toward the scene of the incident.

"No, I didn't see her fall, but when I discovered the body, I asked Kiki to call 911." Kiki, who was standing next to Bishop, shook the officer's hand as he said, "That's right, officer."

Minnehan was taking notes on a small pad. "And what is your name, sir?"

"Michael Bishop."

"The way the body was situated, it wasn't visible from the path. How did you happen to notice that she was down there?" His tone was matter-of-fact, not skeptical or threatening in any way.

"Well, my dog got loose and began running this way. I started after him, but Kiki actually grabbed him just before that short bridge. Max wouldn't settle down and kept focusing on that spot, so I decided to have a look at what was bothering him." After a moment's paused, he added, "I guess he picked up the scent of death."

Bishop didn't even give a thought to the fact that dogs were not allowed on the path or that he was subject to a fine. Apparently, it did not occur to Minnehan, or if it did, it seemed so irrelevant in light of what had happened as not to be worth mentioning.

"Did you happen to know the victim?" Most likely, he asked that question simply because it was the prudent thing to do. He clearly perked up as Bishop answered.

"As a matter of fact, I did. I taught her in high school some fifteen years ago. Her name is Amy Walsh."

The officer's questions now took a different tone and direction. "When was the last time that you saw her alive?"

In Bishop's peripheral vision, he picked up several insects buzzing around. Firmly gripping Max's leash with one hand, he casually swatted the annoying pests away. As he was about to answer the officer's question, he felt a sharp sting on his left hand. He brushed it off and began to explain.

"Actually, I bumped into her after all these years at the Belvedere Inn yesterday. "I went in looking for a …" At that point, he felt that his hand was on fire. A bright red rash had begun to creep up from his hand to his arm, and the area began to swell rapidly. The pesky insects must have been bees that were all over the flowering wild rose bushes that were abundant along both sides of the path. He had only a few moments before he would go into anaphylactic shock. He knew because it had happened before, and the doctors told him that the next time could be worse.

His body began to shake as he forgot the question that he was about to answer. Kiki grabbed him and the dog as Bishop slumped back to the bench. "Epi ... pen ..." was all he could say as he fought the venom invading his body.

***

Lying naked under heavy blankets, his whole body shook from the effects of the shot of adrenaline that he had been given. Several nurses hovered around him as they monitored his vital signs. One of them held his hand as she said softly, "You're going to be fine, Mr. Bishop."

He had gone into anaphylactic shock once before, so he had some idea of what was happening. He knew that the nurse was right. They had reversed the effects of the bee sting. As the shivering began to subside, he asked, "Where am I?"

"You're in the emergency room at York General Hospital."

"What time is it?"

The nurse glanced over her shoulder to a large round clock on the wall which Bishop had failed to notice.

"It's almost 2 in the afternoon."

He struggled to formulate a sentence. "Max ... my dog ... I left ..."

"Don't worry about him." She smiled at him reassuringly. He squinted to read the identification tag that dangled around her neck … Jessica Weaver, R.N. "There's a man in the lobby who is taking good care of him."

"A man?" Bishop was trying to think of the man's name. He had chased down Max when he had run onto the Marginal Way. Then his eyes opened widely, and he tried to lift himself off of the bed.

The nurse held him back. "I'm afraid you're not ready to get up just yet. Do you need to use the restroom?"

"No, no," he shook his head. "It's Amy. Where's Amy? She was lying there …" He stopped mid-sentence as he recalled the feeling of helplessness seeing her lying there. He looked as if he might cry.

Jessica knew that Mr. Bishop had been on the scene of a terrible accident on the Marginal Way when he was stung. She tried to comfort him by saying, "I'm sure that they did everything they could."

The tension left his body as he lowered his head back to the pillow. The shaking had subsided significantly. He looked into the nurse's eyes as he said with resignation, "There wasn't anything they could do. She was dead when I saw her."

The nurse gently brushed his cheek. "Try to get some rest. The doctor should be in to see you soon."

Bishop closed his eyes. He knew that physically he would be back to normal the next day. However, the memory of what happened to Amy Walsh would stay with him forever. He didn't think his day could get much worse until a man came into his cubicle. It wasn't the doctor. It was Officer Minnehan.

***

He was still wearing his uniform, but he had removed his hat to reveal his closely cropped prematurely gray hair. "Mr. Bishop?" He wasn't sure if the old man was asleep or just resting. When Bishop sat up, he continued, "The doc said it was all right for me to come in."

Was the officer about to finc him for letting Max on the path? Considering all that had happened, that would be rather petty. He deserved the fine, but didn't the officer have something better to do? In fact, he did.

Minnehan stood near the foot of the bed as he pulled a pad of paper from his shirt pocket. "I just need to ask you a few more questions about the victim."

It bothered Bishop that he referred to her as the "victim" as if she were unknown. "What do you want to know about Amy Walsh?" he said emphasizing that she had a name.

"When was the last time you saw her alive?"

Bishop thought that he had explained that to the officer before the bee stung him, but he couldn't remember that clearly, so he explained that he had gone to the Belvedere where Amy was the manager looking for accommodations for the week. The Belvedere didn't allow pets, but Amy was kind enough to help him find other accommodations.

Minnehan listened but wasn't taking notes. His interest lay elsewhere.

"Did you come to Ogunquit to see her, Mr. Bishop?"

"Of course not," he said somewhat defensively. "Why would you ask a question like that?"

"Just trying to get a complete picture, sir." After a short pause, he resumed his questioning. "Where were you this morning at about 7 a.m.?"

"I was still at the cottage that I'm renting."

"Anyone who can verify that?"

"Just Max," he said sarcastically.

"Max?" he asked with interest as he began to write the name down.

"Max is my Jack Russell terrier." Then he looked at the officer directly and asked, "Why would I need someone to verify my whereabouts this morning?"

"Based on the evidence that we've gathered so far, we have reason to believe that Ms. Walsh's fall wasn't an accident."

"What?"

"We've examined the area carefully. There's no evidence that she slipped or tripped. We'll wait for an official report from the coroner, but we have to consider the possibility that she was pushed to her death."

To think that Amy died in a tragic accident was bad enough; to consider the possibility that she had been murdered was almost too much for him to handle.

"Who would do such a thing?" he asked incredulously.

"That's why I'm here," Minnehan said soberly.

"Have you been on the Marginal Way since your arrival here yesterday other than when you discovered the body?"

"No," he answered abruptly.

"Do you own a Tilley hat, Mr. Bishop?"

"Well, yes and no," he said with some embarrassment. "I do own a Tilley, but I lost it or misplaced it yesterday. Why do you ask?"

The officer reached into a bag on the floor and pulled out an evidence bag. "We found this near the body." The bag contained a Tilley hat, but Bishop reminded him that they all looked alike.

"Except this one has the initials 'MJB' printed clearly under the back of the brim. Those are your initials, aren't they, Mr. Bishop?"

***

"Let me see that," Bishop snapped as he reached for the plastic bag.

"Please don't remove it from the bag," Minnehan cautioned.

Bishop looked at the hat and saw the initials that he had printed on it some years ago. As he handed the bag back to the officer, he said, "No need to check for prints. It's my hat. Does this mean that I am a *suspect*?" The very thought of that possibility was absolutely absurd to him. It occurred to him that he might need a lawyer, but since he knew he was innocent, he dismissed that notion.

"Well, sir, you were the one who discovered the body, your hat was found at the scene, you admit to knowing the victim, and that you had contact with her yesterday." Minnehan's eyes narrowed as he honed in on his target.

The effects of the sting and its subsequent treatment had faded considerably. Bishop easily countered the accusations. "I've already told you that the only reason I was on that path in the first place was that my dog had run off in that direction. You can check with the staff of Bessie's Restaurant that I called this morning to ask if anyone had turned my hat in. Anyone could have taken it from the shelf where I had placed it when I had dinner there last night. That's circumstantial, at best. Other than our brief meeting yesterday which was very cordial, I hadn't seen Amy since she graduated from high school."

Minnehan took a deep breath as he considered his next step. "How long are you going to be in town?"

"Until Saturday. Why do you ask?"

"I wouldn't plan on going anywhere. I may need to talk with you again," he replied without elaborating. He took down the cottage address and Bishop's cell phone number. He also asked Bishop for his home address and social security number.

"Why do you need all of that?"

"Just want to run it through the database. Routine stuff."

Bishop promised to stop by the police station the next day.

A doctor entered the cubicle. "How are we doing?"

The question was directed at Bishop, but Minnehan answered. "Almost done." He turned back to ask one more question of Bishop who at that point was hungry, tired, and annoyed. "How well do you know Kiki?"

"Not well at all. I left a bag of groceries at Hannaford's this morning, and he came out to the parking lot to hand it to me. When Max got away from me, I'm lucky that Kiki was there to track him down. I don't even know his last name."

"Cavendish," he said as he flipped his notepad shut, muttered his thanks to the doctor, and left.

Chapter Five

After cautioning Bishop to carry his Epipen with him at all times, the doctor released him, and advised him to take it easy for a day or two. After getting dressed, he had to fill out a number of forms since he had been rushed into the emergency room on arrival. He briefly worried about how much of the bill his insurance would pay and how much he would have to pay out of pocket. The expenses of this vacation were adding up, and he been in Ogunquit less than twenty-four hours.

He thanked his nurse, Jessica, for her kindness and went out to the waiting room where he found Max enjoying the attention of several youngsters.

"How are you feeling?" Kiki asked as he stood up to greet the man with whom he had been unintentionally connected for the last few hours.

"I'm fine, really. I can't thank you enough for what you've done for me today." He thought of offering him some money, but realized that he had been on a walk when Max got away from him. His wallet, car keys, and cell phone were all back at the cottage.

"No problem. Glad I could help. Well, I think I'll be on my way." Max was very attentive to his owner, sniffing his clothes, and licking his hand, sensing that something was not right. Kiki reached down to say goodbye to the dog, and then reached out to shake Bishop's hand. "I'm sorry about your friend," he said with sincere feeling. "What an awful way to go."

Bishop had to agree with that sentiment. It was especially awful if, as Minnehan suggested, she was pushed to her death. He thought of the words of Ulysses in the poem by Alfred, Lord Tennyson. Even as an old man, Ulysses was determined "to strive, to seek, to find, and not to yield." Bishop resolved to get to the truth of Amy's death, and he intended to complete his task before the week was out. The fact that he was in the eyes of the police, a "person of interest," had no bearing on his decision. He was doing this for Amy.

Before Kiki left, it occurred to him that Bishop didn't have his car. "Do you need a ride somewhere?"

"No, thanks. You've done enough. I'll just call a cab."

"Well, take care. Maybe I'll see you around during the week."

"I wouldn't be surprised," said Bishop lightheartedly. Before the young man could leave, Bishop called after him. "Did Minnehan talk to you at all?"

"Yeah, he asked me some questions, but I guess I wasn't much help. I didn't see the body." After a short pause, he added, "I've never even met the woman."

"He seems to think that someone pushed Amy to her death, and right now, that someone seems to be me."

"I saw the way you reacted when you discovered her body. No way could you have faked that. I know you didn't do it."

***

A hospital volunteer, an older man with a shock of white hair wearing round wire-rimmed glasses that slipped down his sunburned

45

nose, waited with Bishop at the front entrance until the traditional yellow car from Coastal Cab pulled up. The driver, a man with long gray hair pulled backed in a ponytail and a bushy beard, leaned out of the open window and said, "Make sure that mutt doesn't leave a mess back there." Bishop opened the back door, let Max jump in, and gave the driver his address as he buckled himself in. He also explained that he would need to run in to grab his wallet before he could pay. The driver made eye contact with Bishop through his rear view mirror but said nothing as he pulled away from the curb. The few people that he had met so far in Ogunquit had been quite friendly. Perhaps this guy didn't like dogs. Perhaps he was just trying to be funny. Perhaps he was having a bad day. However bad it might have been, it couldn't have been worse than the day he was having.

Bishop and Max looked out of the window as the cab made its way down Route 1. Fortunately, the driver was not playing the radio. The silence was occasionally interrupted by brief squawky communications from the dispatcher. As they neared his destination, the driver asked, "Did you hear about the accident on the Marginal Way?"

He was somewhat startled by the unexpected question. "Accident?"

"Yeah, some broad went over the edge. Maybe she was drunk." He shrugged his shoulders as if to suggest his inability to care more deeply.

46

He felt like telling the driver that that wasn't "some broad." That was Amy Walsh, and she wasn't drunk. She was jogging when someone for some reason pushed her to her death, and he was determined to find out who did it and why. He wasn't about to inform the driver that he was "a person of interest" in that incident. Instead, he simply said, "Really? That's so sad."

He wondered why the rumor mill had Amy's death as an accident when the police were clearly looking at it as a homicide. It wasn't until he spoke with Officer Minnehan the next day that the reason for that became clear.

***

After taking a long hot shower, he had some cereal and a banana for lunch. He took a cup of hot tea with him as he went out on the second floor patio to relax. With the sun now facing the back of the cottage, he sat in an old wicker chair, put his feet up on the small ottoman, and set his cup on the oval glass-topped side table to his right. Rather than trying to read, he immersed himself in his surroundings. The view from this vantage point was so calming that he briefly considered inquiring at Littleford Realty what properties in this neighborhood might be on the market.

He quickly dismissed the idea. He did want to talk to Martha Littleford and Kelli as well but not about real estate. They knew Amy. Perhaps they would have some idea of who might have wanted to see her dead. From the bits and pieces of the phone conversation that he had overheard the day before, Amy and Martha were not exactly the best of friends. He wanted to know why.

47

He also recalled a conversation that Amy had with someone when he had first arrived at the Belvedere. It sounded as though she had fired that person. What was his name? Bishop's memory failed him. He tried to excuse that failure on the fact that the name didn't seem important at the time. He tried to remember by going through the alphabet. It was a technique that sometimes worked. Adam … Brad … Chris … Dan … not Dan … David. That seemed right. Amy had proudly told him that she was the manager of the inn. There had to be an assistant manager. That was another person with whom he planned to talk, and that person would know David if that was, in fact, his name.

***

When Ron arrived, Max greeted him with his usual exuberance, a burst of energy that lasted for a few moments as Bishop shook his friend's hand.

Jennings looked around his new home for the next few days. He plunked his suitcase on the tiled foyer. "Cool place! How did you find this?"

"Long story," he replied truthfully. While Bishop showed Ron around, he asked, "How was your drive?"

"Great, until I got on the New Hampshire pike and the speed limit jumped to 75."

Bishop had an idea of what was coming. Jennings had a heavy foot and tended to drive his Nissan Sentra as if it were the sports car that he couldn't afford. "Get a ticket?"

"Yup. I got nailed going 87 just a couple of miles before the Piscataqua Bridge. That's gonna set me back a few bucks," he said with a smile. "How was your first full day at the beach?"

"Long story," he said again. As he thought about it, it was still hard for him to believe. "I had an encounter with the police as well," he said cryptically.

Jennings looked shocked. He couldn't imagine what his friend might have done. "Are you gonna tell me, or what?" He asked with a mixture of curiosity and concern.

"Why don't we grab something for dinner, and I'll bring you up to speed?"

"Good. I'm starving." Ron might have stopped on the road for something to eat only an hour or two earlier, but he would still be starving. The man had an uncanny ability to eat just about anything and everything at any time and not gain weight.

"How about a pizza?"

"Sounds good to me."

As they walked to La Pizzeria on Main Street, Bishop began to relay the events of this unfortunate and unforgettable day. Amy Walsh was unknown to Ron as she had graduated a few years before Jennings arrived at Trinity. They bobbed and weaved as people walked the other way, some paying more attention to their phones than to where they were going. Most of the time, they walked side by side. Ron listened and refrained from interrupting with the many questions swirling in his head. When Bishop finished his narrative,

Ron looked at him with a mixture of disbelief, sympathy, and concern.

"What are you going to do?"

They entered the pizza place and found a booth near the back of the small dining area. After the waitress dropped off their menus, he looked directly at Ron and whispered, "If Amy was murdered, and I'm convinced that she was, I'm going to find out who did it before the police decide to arrest me." Given Bishop's recent successes working as an amateur sleuth with Lieutenant Hodge of the Groveland Police Department, Ron had faith that his friend would do just that.

***

When the pizza and beer arrived, both men devoted themselves to the task at hand. Bishop anticipated taking the leftovers back to the cottage, but Ron's king-sized appetite eliminated that possibility. As they sat back to enjoy the remaining beer, Bishop brought up the phone call that Ron had received from Sister Estelle that prompted Ron's spur-of-the-moment decision to join his friend in Ogunquit.

"Did you call Blake to get his take on Estelle's decision?" His report on the shortcomings of both Sisters Ann and Pat had been instrumental in their suspension.

"As a matter of fact I did after I calmed down a bit," Ron said as he looked at his empty plate. He pushed it to the side for the waitress to pick up. "She didn't consult with him or even inform him of her change of heart. He was ripping mad and said that he might resign."

Bishop raised his eyebrows at that possibility. "I hope you tried to talk him out of it."

"I did. Blake's a good guy. I certainly don't want him to quit. I mean … he has a family to consider."

"I hope you informed Sister Ann of your decision to take some vacation time."

"Of course I did. I left her a detailed memo, but basically, everything is already set for the new school year. She just has to keep the seat warm."

"That's Sister Pat's specialty," quipped Bishop.

"No doubt."

"Have you heard anything about her lately?" Sister Pat had been ordered to rethink her vocation as a member of the Sisters of the Holy Rosary, but Bishop wasn't convinced that the school had seen the last of her.

"No," Ron said with a sigh of relief, "and I don't want to, either."

"Did you tell Terry you were coming up here?"

He smacked his forehead. "Jeez! No! I was in such a hurry to pull everything together, I didn't think to do that." Then he added with a self-deprecating chuckle, "I'm lucky I remembered to call Mary Ellen!"

Just then the waitress arrived, and left the check on the table as she picked up the pizza pan and the dishes. "No hurry," she smiled as she left.

Bishop went to pick up the check, but Ron grabbed it first. "Oh no," he said as he pulled a credit card from his wallet. "You're letting me stay at that beautiful place. The least I can do is pick up the meal tabs."

"I want you to do more than that," Bishop said in a serious tone.

Ron was a bit confused. "I can help with the rent, too," he offered.

"That's not what I meant," he answered cryptically.

Ron's face was a blank. "Then, what do you want me to do?"

"I want you to help me find Amy's killer."

Neither man spoke. Bishop wanted to return the spot where he had discovered the body, but it was getting dark. The real work would begin tomorrow.

Chapter Six

It didn't take long for Ron to start to feel at home, especially in the kitchen. After calling Mary Ellen and giving her a brief summary of all that transpired that day, he grabbed some chips, salsa, and a soda and turned on the flat screen television in the living room. Reclining on the sectional sofa, he flipped through the channels looking for a ballgame. In this part of the country, there was a strong animosity towards the Mets and the Yankees. This was Red Sox Nation, and since the Sox were losing 1 – 0 to the Indians in the sixth inning, he settled in to watch them lose.

Bishop was very tired, but still rattled by the day's events largely here in Ogunquit, but to some extent also the return of Sister Ann back in Groveland, he decided to check his email while keeping an eye on the game. When the message popped up that he needed a password to join a network, he remembered that Kelli had given him one when he was at her office. A degree of panic set in as he tried to recall what he had done with that information. He went into his bedroom, found the rental papers, sifted through them and found the password. Relieved, he went back into the living room and gave that information to Ron before he had a chance to forget to do that.

After logging in, he found that most of the emails were of the junk variety; others needed a response that could wait until later. The one email that caught his attention was from Terry Mortensen, the office secretary at Holy Trinity. If some people had a nose for news and others had an ear for gossip, Terry had both. From her desk, she delighted in picking up both news and gossip. It made her otherwise boring job much more interesting, but what she enjoyed most was sharing what she knew with her closest friends. As he read her message, Ron reacted to what was happening in Boston.

David Ortiz had stepped to the plate with two men on. "Be careful with this guy," Ron said to the Indians' pitcher who couldn't afford to walk him and load the bases. Next he heard the voice of Don Orsillo, the Red Sox broadcaster, "Ortiz hits a long fly to deep right … That ball is gone! … Big Papi just put the Sox on top 3 – 1 with his 27th homer of the year!" The pandemonium in the stands wasn't matched by Ron's frustration. "They gave him a pitch right down the heart of the plate."

Bishop rather liked Ortiz since he was still at the top of his game as one of the oldest players in the league. He felt an affinity of sorts with players such as Ortiz and the even-older Bartolo Colon of the Mets.

"I've got something else you're not going to believe," he said to his younger friend.

"What do you mean?" asked Ron, still obviously annoyed by that homerun.

"I got an email from Terry with a few tidbits from Sister Ann's first day back at the helm."

"Oh, my God!" he said as he playfully covered his ears.

"It's not that bad," as he glanced through the message once again. "Apparently, Sister Ann walked into the main office first thing this morning as if she hadn't been suspended and spent the last few months working in a shelter for battered women. Terry was shocked when she saw her, but she managed to say, 'Nice to see you, Sister.'"

"Reasonable enough," commented Ron as he grabbed another handful of chips.

Bishop decided to give Ron a little quiz to see how well he knew the woman for whom he worked. "How do you think she responded to Terry's greeting?"

The assistant principal took almost no time to offer a few possibilities. "Nice to see you, too."

"Nope."

"Glad to be back."

"Nope."

"I've learned a lot over the past few months."

Bishop raised his eyebrows in disbelief. "Three strikes. Those are the kinds of responses that you or I might make. You need to try to think like her."

"I'm glad I *don't* think like her. Okay, tell me what she said when Terry said, 'Nice to see you.'"

"She said, 'Thank you,' and walked back to her office."

Ron almost choked on his soda as he burst into laughter. "You've got to be kidding me."

"I don't think that Terry could make that up."

When he regained his composure, Ron asked, "Did Terry report anything else interesting?"

As a matter of fact she had, but Bishop debated whether or not to tell his friend. After hesitating for a moment, he decided to tell him because he would find out sooner or later anyway.

"She took down your display from the bulletin board outside the main office," he said softly as if that would soften the blow.

He jumped up from sofa. "She what?"

"She removed the display."

"But why?" he said in exasperation.

"You don't expect me to justify her actions, do you?" He was trying to lighten the mood without much success.

"When the Student Council was stuck for ideas, I helped them come up with 'Reach for the Stars' as a theme for the year. What could be wrong with that?" He shrugged his shoulders as he lifted his open hands in bewilderment.

"There's nothing wrong with it," Bishop pointed out, "except that Sister Ann didn't come up with it. You did. I think it's her way of saying, 'I'm back, and I'm in charge.'"

Ron nodded in agreement. It was likely the first volley in what could be a series of skirmishes all year long. Even after his long drive, he still wasn't sleepy, so he grabbed some ice cream from the fridge, and settled back on the sofa to watch the rest of the game.

Bishop sent a quick message to Terry. He appreciated her update, and urged her to feel free to call or text him at any time. He refrained from telling her about his day in an email. He also was concerned that certain individuals might get wind of his situation. He was so tired that he decided to go to bed even though he knew that no lead was safe at Fenway Park. The final score really didn't matter to him. He had other worries. He planned to walk the Marginal Way early the next morning. Was it possible that he could find some clue to solving Amy's death that the police had overlooked? Might there have been a witness who had yet to come forward? Who had taken his Tilley hat and planted it at the scene of the crime? What were the chances that finding the hat there was merely coincidence?

As he drifted off to sleep, other questions surfaced, certainly not as urgent, but nonetheless troubling. How had Sister Ann managed to convince Sister Estelle to let her return as the head administrator of Holy Trinity? Was she truly contrite? Was she a changed person? Given what he heard of her first day back, it was possible, but unlikely. Why would Sister Estelle have had a last minute change of heart? Why would she ignore the evidence gathered by Blake Driscoll? Did Sister Ann have some leverage to use against Sister Estelle? If so, what could it be?

* * *

With the first light of day, Bishop was up. He took care of Max, had a glass of orange juice, and quietly headed out the door. Ron was still sleeping. Maybe that game last night had gone into extra innings. He didn't expect to be out for long.

Instead of walking down Israel Head Road to the Marginal Way, he went up Shore Road so that he could enter the path at a more northern point. He would have been wearing his Tilley if it weren't for the fact that the Ogunquit Police had it in a plastic bag as a possible piece of evidence. With no wind to speak of, the water looked more like that of a lake. Many of the small waves made little noise as they rolled toward the shore. Unlike the previous morning with its think fog, there wasn't a cloud in the sky. The rising sun shimmered on the rippled surface, promising a warm day ahead.

One side of the walkway to this entrance to the Marginal Way bordered an upscale inn whose grounds were lined by an explosion of dazzling flowers. Mesmerized by the landscape before him, Bishop recalled lines from "Tintern Abbey," a poem by the 18th Century English poet, William Wordsworth. "Once again," he wrote, "Do I behold these steep and lofty cliffs." He had returned to the banks of the Wye River whose beauty had given him much pleasure in the past. He suggests that the mere recollection of that beauty has sustained him through many dark days in the intervening years. "How oft in spirit have I turned to thee,/ O sylvan Wye!" Furthermore, he believes that his present experience with nature will sustain him in the future. "Therefore am I still/ A lover of the meadows and the woods/ And mountains." The Marginal Way had in years past brought much joy to Bishop, and that was the reason that he finally decided to return. However, in order for his present visit to bring him comfort in the future, his thoughts returned to the task at hand. He knew that he would need to settle the question of what had happened to his former student, Amy Walsh.

This then was more than a pleasure walk. He was looking for something … anything … that might lead him to the truth of her senseless death. As he made his way along the path, it occurred to him that approximately twenty-four hours earlier, Amy had done the same thing. There was, however, one major difference … she never reached the end of the path. Who or what had caused her to fall to her death? Had she arranged to meet someone? Assuming that she had been murdered, he wondered if she knew her assailant, or had her murder been a random act?

He encountered a middle-aged woman who had set up an easel on a dry flat rock just off the trail. She was totally absorbed in her painting of the rocky shore below. At her feet was a box containing her supplies. Wearing a floppy hat, and a painter's smock over light blue slacks, she held a brush in her right hand. The spray of the waves looked as if it was splashing off the canvas. Bishop, who had little artistic talent, said loudly, "You're doing a beautiful job!" Startled, her whole body tensed as she turned her head from her work to take the measure of this man. Was she aware of what had happened to Amy the previous morning? Was she fearful that he was the perpetrator seeking his next victim?

Bishop realized just how easy it would have been for someone to approach Amy on the path unaware. He waved to the woman and smiled, trying to deescalate the situation as he said, "I'm so sorry if I startled you."

"It's not your fault," she said graciously.

The possibility that this woman had been in this very spot twenty-four hours earlier prompted him to question her. "Do you come here every morning?" he asked conversationally.

"No," she laughed lightly, "this area is an artist's heaven. I am never at a loss for places that I want to paint. I've been working on this one for about a week," she said as she gestured back to the canvas.

"Were you here yesterday?"

"No, it was too foggy to get anything done. How about yourself?" It was as clear from her question that she was aware of what had happened here.

"Unfortunately, I was." He realized that his name was probably all over the news this morning, so he had nothing to hide. He added, "My name is Michael Bishop. I was the one who found her." The image of Amy's eyes staring blankly up at the sky suddenly flashed before him.

"Oh, I'm so sorry!" she said compassionately. At a loss for what else to say, she added, "My name is Megan Fleming. I live in South Berwick, but I come here often."

"Pleased to meet you." Bishop, trying to shake yesterday's memory away, looked down at the paved path that was cracked and broken in places. He scraped some sand to the edge of the pavement with his sneaker.

"What a terrible accident," she offered, breaking the silence.

Accident? Yesterday, Officer Minnehan strongly hinted at the possibility of foul play, and Bishop was a person of interest. Confused, he asked, "Accident? Is that what the newspapers are calling it?"

She glanced seaward, perhaps judging how much time she had left to work before conditions changed. "I don't know about that. There are a couple of weeklies in this area, one out of Wells on

Wednesdays and one out of York on Fridays, but it made the TV news out of Portland last night."

"I should let you get back to your work," he said apologetically. "Nice to have met you, Megan. Have a nice day," he added as he resumed his walk along the Marginal Way. The sun was getting stronger, and here he was without sunglasses or a hat. He thought his sunglasses might still be in his car; he knew where his hat was … still in the possession of the Ogunquit Police. He needed to buy something inexpensive to get him through the week, but he had more urgent matters on his mind.

***

The first few hundred yards of the walkway had a protective green chain link fence. Although it marred the natural beauty, it was obviously deemed necessary. At other places along the way, there were some barriers in place where there is a precipitous drop to the rocks below. From certain places, it was possible to leave the path and carefully descend to the rocky areas left relatively dry even at high tide. Megan, the painter that he had just met, had positioned herself on one such outcropping. These spots were ideal for those intent on searching for shells and small stones. Bishop spotted a small cairn, wondering who had assembled that tribute and how long it had stood there. At low tide, there were some small sandy stretches where one could catch a true sea-level view.

As he continued his walk, he tried to pay attention to where he was stepping as well as to what was around him. Even though he remembered to bring along his Epipen, he was especially wary of the increasingly active bees on the numerous blossoms. He came across some large rocks and many smaller ones along the edge of the path. Was it possible that Amy accidentally tripped over one of them? He didn't recall seeing any rocks near the bridge where he had discovered the body, but he couldn't rely on his memory. Another fifteen minutes of uninterrupted walking would bring him to that spot.

Although the path was about five feet wide, in places it was narrower because of branches and bushes on either side reaching out as if to close the path to intruders. Some of the trees on the ocean side were easily twenty feet tall, obscuring the view in places. On the other side, many of the owners of the homes with the multi-million dollar views used hedges or their own fencing to achieve some degree of privacy. Bishop wondered whether anyone living in one of those homes saw or heard anything unusual the previous morning.

Wanting to take a breather, he sat at one of the thirty-nine benches that line the footpath. They were strategically placed to allow one to linger at some of the most scenic spots. He sat at bench #8 and realized when he looked around that if he had started his walk by coming straight down Israel Head Road, he would have entered the path here. In addition to the numbers, the benches had small bronze plates on them with the names of those in whose memory they were dedicated. Not only was it a wonderful tribute to those who loved this area, it also served as a source of funding needed to maintain this gem for future generations.

Sitting there, it was easy for him to drift back to a time when Grace was by his side walking that same path. They must have walked back and forth between Ogunquit Beach and Perkins Cove hundreds of times over the years. When they encountered walkers or joggers coming from the opposite direction, she would slip ahead of him. Once the path was open again, he would catch up to her, and they would resume a conversation or stop to watch the waves crash against the rocks.

Sometimes they would spot a loon floating on the water, waiting for it to dive below the surface. They would each look to the spot where they expected it to surface, laughing when the loon proved both of them wrong. Bishop enjoyed photography, and he had taken many photos along this stretch of internationally known coastline. The stunning views of sea and sky also served as a backdrop for many photos of his beautiful wife. It seemed as though time stood still, but of course, it hadn't. Grace was gone, but he didn't need a photo album to remember her vividly.

As he resumed his walk, he encountered the famous lighthouse. Many tourists might have wondered about the wisdom of placing such a small structure at this location. Had they stopped to read the accompanying placards, they would have realized that the structure was, in fact, a working pumping station for Ogunquit. The Friends of the Marginal Way had decided that the lighthouse exterior was more appealing than that of the pump itself. Over the years, that group had been responsible for raising the funds to repair the path after several damaging storms, evidence of the increasing threat posed by global warming which only the uniformed refused to acknowledge.

Walking farther along the path, he approached the footbridge where he had discovered the body of his former student with an assist from his wayward dog, Max. It was still quite early on this weekday morning near the end of August, and only infrequently did he encounter another walker. Suddenly, he was fully alert. Mere yards ahead, he saw the legs of a person prone on the ground at the side of the path. Had there been another murder? Would Officer Minnehan believe for a moment that it was mere coincidence that he had discovered another body? Was there a serial killer in Ogunquit?

Chapter Seven

Just as he began to pull out his cell phone to call 911, the legs began to move. A man whom Bishop judged to be about thirty years old stood up. He was barefoot, and wearing a blue bandanna that covered the top of his head, and a tee shirt with an American flag design. His left shoulder displayed the stars on a blue background and the rest of the shirt had horizontal red and white stripes. He put something in the pocket of his cutoff jeans, glanced briefly in Bishop's direction, and walked away from the footbridge at a rapid pace. The veteran teacher did not know who this man was or what he had been doing there before he arrived on the scene. Although generally good at remembering faces, he was somewhat rattled and wasn't sure that he would recognize him if he ever saw him again. His wraparound reflective sunglasses all but eliminated an easy identification.

When Bishop crossed the short span of the footbridge, he realized that the man must have been seated on the ground, leaning against one of the wooden posts that supported the bridge, with his legs outstretched. What was he doing there? Was he merely resting? Was he enjoying the quiet that Bishop interrupted? Did he know that this was the spot from which Amy fell to her death? What was it that he placed in his pocket? Why had he stared at Bishop and walked away without saying a word?

There were no markers indicating that this was still an active crime scene. Anyone walking by today would have no idea that a tragic event had taken place here. That saddened him. Looking toward the west, he realized that there was no house with a direct line of sight to this spot. In fact, that side of the path was lined with thick bushes and some taller trees. They would have provided a natural cover for an assailant. Examining the other side of the path, he saw no evidence of loose stones or rocks that might have caused an accidental fall. However, that stretch immediately after the footbridge did have a rather steep slope leading to the black jagged rocks and the sea below. Conceivably, if Amy lost her balance or lost consciousness, she might have rolled down the sandy embankment, then hit the rocks, tumbling into the huge crevice in which she had been found. Someone also might have shoved her off of the footpath where she hit her head on the rocks, and then dragged the body to the crevice, assuming incorrectly that at high tide all evidence of the crime would be washed out to sea. The normal extent of high tide was evident by a mere glance at the rocks. Darker rocks were underwater at high tide; lighter rocks were not. The demarcation line was so even along this stretch that it seemed as though someone had painted it on the rocks. Of course, storm surges could alter that pattern significantly.

His search of the surrounding area yielded no clues. That really didn't surprise him that much. He assumed that the authorities had done a thorough job. They did, after all, recover his hat at the scene. His mind kept drifting back to the horrible image of Amy's blank stare. Why hadn't anyone brought flowers here? Certainly, many people knew what had happened. The cabbie knew. Megan, the artist, knew. Yet, no one had attempted to create a makeshift memorial of any kind.

Bishop thought of the words of the English Romantic poet, John Keats, who knowing that he was dying at the age of twenty-six, instructed that these words be inscribed on his tombstone: *Here lies one whose name was writ in water.* Keats sadly and wrongly assumed that his poetry would be forgotten, and that it would be as if he had never lived at all. A name written in water disappears as it is written. Would the life of Amy Walsh be forgotten? Bishop was determined to make sure that that did not happen. She deserved that much.

Rather than finish walking the path to Perkins Cove, he headed back the way he had come. There had to be answers to the many questions surrounding her death, and he was determined to get to them.

***

When he entered the cottage, he was greeted by Max and by the aroma of frying bacon coming from the kitchen.

"Just in time for breakfast," Ron said as he waved a pair of tongs in the air. As he flipped the sizzling strips in the pan, he asked, "How was your walk?"

Bishop sat at the kitchen table and gave Max some needed attention. "I walked the Marginal Way to the spot where Amy fell to her death hoping that I might find some clue as to what really happened."

"Any luck?" Ron asked as he deftly cracked an egg into a bowl with one hand.

Impressed with his friend's culinary skills, he commented, "I didn't know you were such a good cook."

Ron laughed as he replied, "Yeah, well, let's keep that between us."

Bishop nodded his agreement. "I did come upon a man who was sitting at the edge of the footbridge, but as I approached, he put something in his pocket, gave me an odd look, and took off."

"Know who he is?"

"No, but I hope to find out..." he said as Jennings set two plates of bacon, eggs, and toast on the table "... among other things."

Over breakfast and cups of green tea, they settled on a plan for the rest of the morning. Ron agreed to take Max for a walk on Main Street while he looked for a replacement for Bishop's Tilley hat and engage a few shopkeepers in small talk about Amy's death. After bringing Max back to the cottage, he would meet Bishop for lunch at Bessie's at 1:00 p.m.

Over the years, the seventy-one-year-old English teacher had given some thought to the prospect of writing mystery novels after he retired. Although he had yet to retire, he recently found himself in the middle of solving several real-life mysteries. The fact that he was considered a person of interest in the suspicious death of his former student was more than enough motivation to once again assume his role as amateur sleuth. He decided to check in with Officer

68

Minnehan on the progress of the investigation. He also planned on stopping by Littleford Realty and the Belvedere Inn to talk with anyone who knew Amy.

Before either man had a chance to leave, Ron received a text from Terry, the school secretary. With a confused expression on his face, he read the brief message out loud: *"Jeff White and his parents just went into Sister Ann's office ... more later."*

Bishop had never taught the young man, but he had heard the name a number of times and not in a very complimentary way. "What's that all about?"

"I have no idea," replied Ron. "After an incident at an end-of-the-year school party and with failing grades in three core subjects, I made it clear to Jeff and his parents that he would have to transfer to another school."

"Did they understand the basis of your decision?"

"They certainly did," he said emphatically as he recalled the conversation. "They weren't too happy, but I didn't expect them to be. Why would they be meeting with Sister Ann?"

Bishop had a hunch about what might be going on, but he preferred to keep it to himself. Why upset Ron unnecessarily? Although he knew the principal well, there was always the possibility that her suspension had changed her. At any rate, with Terry's antennae up, they would know more soon enough.

"Perhaps they're just there to pick up his transcript," offered Bishop.

"Yeah ... maybe," answered Ron, clearly unconvinced.

***

The police station was located in the Community Center on School Street, just off Shore Road. Bishop, wearing light gray shorts and a pale blue chambray shirt, asked the attendant at the desk if Officer Minnehan was available.

"Your name, please?" asked the young African American woman whose hair was braided in cornrows tight to her scalp.

"Michael Bishop."

"Is he expecting you, Mr. Bishop?"

"No, but I'm sure he knows who am I," he replied with a smile.

"Empty your pockets in this bin, please, and walk through right here," she said as she gestured to the screening device. Bishop placed his cottage key, his cell phone, and his wallet in the bin. He realized that he had forgotten to take his Epipen with him. Not following doctor's orders could get him in a lot of trouble, but he didn't expect to encounter any bees in here. If he were to get stung, it would be by the words of Minnehan.

After a few moments sitting in an uncomfortable, molded-plastic chair in an uncomfortably warm room with one small window overlooking the parking lot, the officer came in. Bishop stood to shake his hand.

"What are you doing here?"

That question puzzled the teacher. He felt like saying, *I'm the person of interest in the death of Amy Walsh, remember?* Instead, he replied, "You told me not to leave town. You took my information yesterday and asked me to stop by today."

"Oh, right. Everything checked out. You're free to do as you wish." He seemed to be in a hurry to get back to whatever he was doing, but Bishop wasn't ready to leave.

"What about my hat?"

"You want your hat? I can have someone bring it down for you," he replied, as he again appeared ready to dismiss him.

"No, I don't want my hat. I could never wear that hat again, but yesterday, you tracked me down in the hospital asking some incriminating questions because my hat was found at the murder scene." He was both relieved and confused by Minnehan's sudden change of heart.

"Murder? Who said it was a murder?" The officer now seemed a bit edgy.

"Well, you didn't use that word, but you certainly implied as much. You also questioned Kiki, the guy that helped me track down my dog."

"Just doing my job," he said with a sigh. He clearly wanted his visitor out of his hair.

Bishop needed to understand the reason for the officer's rapid shift. "May I ask what the coroner's report indicated as cause of death?"

"Not really," he said with a flash of temper, "but I'll tell you anyway. The victim didn't have any wounds other than those caused by the fall. There was no evidence of alcohol or drugs in her system.

There's no evidence of foul play. There's no reason to believe she committed suicide. It was just an unfortunate accident. Now, if you'll excuse me, I have some reports to fill out."

He suddenly remembered seeing Amy's ear buds. "What about her phone?" he asked excitedly. "She was listening to music. Did you recover that phone?"

"Yes, but it was in bad shape … smashed from the fall and water damaged as well." He almost seemed relieved by that. Bishop wondered whether her phone records could be subpoenaed, and realized quickly that that was not going to happen if the police were treating this as an accident.

For a moment, Bishop considered accepting the coroner's judgment. He was no longer a suspect in a murder investigation. That was the good news. On the other hand, Minnehan's initial reaction was that Amy had been pushed to her death. It didn't seem likely that she simply tripped and ended up in that crevice. "An accident?" Bishop asked incredulously. "What about my hat?"

"What about it?"

"I explained to you that I had lost that hat. I think somebody used it in attempt to frame me for her murder."

Minnehan's face reddened as he snapped back. "I told you it was an accident. Now, why can't you just accept that fact and go on about your business?"

"Because I don't believe that it was an accident. Someone's responsible for her death, and I'm going to find out who did it, with or without your help," he said emphatically.

"You're wasting your time."

"Fine. It's my time." Minnehan gestured for Bishop to leave the room. As he walked into the hallway with the officer close behind, he thought back to the questioning that he had been subjected to the day before. Minnehan wanted to know if he knew the victim. He suggested that Bishop might have gotten into an argument with her. He turned back to the officer to ask one last question of his own.

"Officer Minnehan, did you know Amy Walsh?"

He clearly was caught off guard. He flushed again as he mumbled a response. "I knew her from around town ... but I ... I didn't know her very well."

From his many years dealing with students, Bishop had a good feel for when someone was lying. He had that feeling now. Minnehan was hiding something.

***

Max was more than ready to join Ron on his walk into town. Many of the establishments along Main Street were motels, restaurants, or gift shops. Bishop had mentioned that dogs were not allowed on the beach or on the Marginal Way. They were welcome on Main Street, however, as more than one place of business kept bowls of water on the sidewalk for their canine visitors. Max took advantage of each one that he encountered.

After a quick walk through a couple of smaller shops, Ron realized that he might fail in his first assignment. He didn't find any wide-brimmed men's straw hats. He did locate some baseball caps with a large red "B" on a white background. He was tempted to buy one for his friend, a long-time Mets fan, but he wasn't sure that he would see the value of owning a Boston Red Sox cap. Besides, it didn't provide much protection against the strong sun of late August.

For some reason, he found himself attracted to The Village Food Market. As he walked along the aisles, Ron was bombarded with a tantalizing collection of culinary delights. There was a case of deli meats ranging from capicola to prosciutto, a cooler of dozens of cheeses including brie, gouda, and gorgonzola, and trays of fresh breads and rolls. Max was content to sniff politely as Ron debated what he should buy. His decision was complicated when he arrived at the display of desserts. He weighed all of the possibilities carefully before deciding on a slice of black forest cake and two chocolate éclairs. The clerk carefully wrapped each piece in waxed paper and placed them in a bag. Ron planned on eating the cake as soon as he left the store, sharing a small piece with Max. He hoped that Bishop like éclairs; if not, nothing would go to waste.

He could practically taste the black forest cake as he headed outside. Just then, it occurred to him that he hadn't made any headway in the two tasks that Bishop had assigned ... buy a hat and chat up some locals to get their take on Amy's death. Luckily, the morning rush was over, so he walked back to the clerk who had waited on him.

"Excuse me, miss!" This woman had probably been working since six that morning, and as summer's end neared had probably had had her fill of dealing with complaining customers, countless

74

tourists asking the same questions, and the occasional unwelcome advances. Her hair was pulled back, but a few wisps along her temples had escaped which she attempted to push back.

"What can I do for ya, buddy?"

Before answering he looked down at Max who sat next to his right foot without command, hoping perhaps that he would be given something from the bag that Ron was holding. Max, however, had no suggestions on what to say to the clerk.

"I'm looking for a man's summer hat," he blurted out. Ron didn't even look the type that ever wore a hat. "Do you know where I can find one?"

She poured a carafe of water into the coffee machine behind the counter, then smiled. "Usually, people ask me when the next trolley will be coming by. A man's hat? That's a new one."

"No, I'm serious. My friend lost his hat and wanted me to pick one up for him." He knew that his story was sounding stranger and stranger, but he thought he was better off starting with the hat before getting to more serious matters. Maybe that was a mistake. What would Bishop think of him for flubbing his first assignment?

"Why don't you buy your friend a Red Sox cap? Half the guys in town wear them."

"He's a Mets fan, I'm afraid." Before she had a chance to suggest that he try to find a Mets cap, he explained the specific type of hat that he was looking for.

She thought for a moment. "A Tilley hat? Sounds kinda pricey." She looked off to the side as if the answer might be written on the labels of the cans of Campbell's soup that lined a nearby shelf. "I'd try the Kittery Trading Post. It's down on Route 1. They have tons of stuff like that."

"Thanks, I'll check that out." He hadn't brought up the question that he really wanted to ask, but he had no reason to linger at the counter, so he let Max lead the way outside. Ron was afraid that Bishop would assign him to Dante's Seventh Circle of Hell if he came up empty in search of town gossip. He had to do something. On his way out of the door, he grabbed a loaf of French bread in a long narrow paper bag. Max seemed a little confused as Ron walked back to the counter.

"I just couldn't resist," he said sheepishly. As she dug his change out of the register, he just blurted out, "Have you heard much talk about the woman who died out on the Marginal Way?" He knew he wouldn't get any points for the subtlety of his interrogation, but he was convinced another customer would walk in any second.

"Surfing?" she asked with interest.

"No, I'm afraid she fell onto the rocks while jogging."

"That's tough. Hadn't heard about it."

Ron thought it strange that she hadn't picked up any hints of gossip. "The Portland news had something on it."

"Honey, when I get home after being on my feet all day, I'm not listening to the news." As she spoke, a woman with three small children stormed into the store. It was time for Ron to leave. He thanked the clerk and wandered down Beach Street. When he was anxious, he ate, so he decided to have one of the two chocolate éclairs. Max waited impatiently for some crumbs to drop. Uncomfortable with Max's appeal for his share, Ron gave him the last bite of cake minus the chocolate and cream.

Returning to the shop with the overpriced, official one-size-fits-all hats, Ron bought one for Bishop. With the investigation now in progress, he figured that his friend wouldn't want to waste time driving to Kittery to track down a Tilley. A hat was a hat. It would at least provide some protection from the sun. It might even help his investigation if people assumed that he was a native. It often seemed to him that Bishop could do just about anything. Maybe he could adopt a Downeast accent before the week was out.

As he made his purchase, he asked the cashier, a young man with a Mohawk and a silver ring in his lower lip, if he had heard about yesterday's accident on the Marginal Way. He gave Ron a blank stare as if he had just asked him to name the capitals of all fifty states. He headed back to the cottage with the remaining pastries, some bread, and a hat, but not even a whisper of a clue as to what happened to Amy.

As he unlocked the front door and let Max scamper toward his favorite spot in the porch, his cell phone buzzed. He had another text from Terry. Jeff White and his parents were headed to the Guidance Office after their conference with the principal. All three seemed to be in a good mood. Ron realized that it was unlikely that they had just stopped by to pick up his transcript. Why had Sister Ann allowed Jeff to return to Trinity? Perhaps she would make him Student Council President for good measure just to show that there were no hard feelings. For the first time in his career, Ron wasn't looking forward to going back to school next week.

Chapter Eight

For the second time since he had arrived in Ogunquit, Bishop walked into the office of Littleford Realty. What he hoped to be a relaxing vacation had turned into a nightmare that he could not have imagined. He had met a former student who saved him from the embarrassment of poor planning by finding him the perfect beach cottage. Within the last twenty-four hours, he had gone from being considered a person of interest in her death to just another tourist. Why was Amy's death now considered merely an accident?

Kelli was seated at her desk as he entered. She was wearing a pale yellow sleeveless top with a gold cross dangling from a thick chain around her neck. "Where's Max?" she asked, clearly disappointed that Bishop was alone.

"A colleague of mine from school came up for a few days, so Max has some company."

"Oh, that must be nice for both of you," she said in a conspiratorial whisper.

Bishop tried to read her tone. What was she implying? Whatever she thought didn't matter. He had more important issues to pursue. "Is Ms. Littleford in?"

"No. She won't be in until after lunch. Probably trying to carve someone up for a few extra bucks ... as if Miss Moneybags needs it. Is there something I can do for you?"

He let the negative comments about her boss pass for the moment. "No, I was just hoping to talk with her ... just wondering if she had any idea who might try to harm Amy."

"Harm her?" She appeared shocked by the notion. "Why would anyone want to harm her? Besides, didn't the police conclude that it was an accident?"

"Yes, apparently they did, but it just doesn't make sense to me. Even if she fell, it's unlikely that she'd end up wedged in that crevice." As he put his hand through what was left of his salt-and-pepper hair, he added, "And someone planted my hat at the scene."

"Really?" she said as her voice edged up an octave. Perhaps for a moment she considered the possibility that she was talking to the perpetrator.

"I left my hat somewhere … not sure where … and someone obviously used it to put the blame elsewhere." Accepting his explanation, her thoughts turned to her friend. "I can't believe that Amy is gone."

"Neither can I. We were going to have lunch one day this week and catch up on old times," he said shaking his head as if he could erase the image of her dead body lying in that crevice with the gulls circling overhead.

She grabbed a tissue from the box on her desk, crumpled it, and dabbed at her nose. "And I feel so guilty!"

Outwardly, Bishop's expression didn't change, but that remark caught him off guard. What was she implying? He decided to say nothing and wait for her to continue.

"We usually jog together every morning on the beach if the tide is low enough and otherwise on the Marginal Way. She did it just to stay in shape, and I … well … I need to lose a few." She smiled sheepishly as she gestured at her rather plump form.

Bishop wanted to keep the focus on what might be important. "Why didn't you go jogging that day?"

"The boss called me Sunday night and told me that she wanted me to be at the office by 7:00 a.m. on Monday. I wouldn't have had time to jog, take a shower, and be here by then."

"Did she say why she wanted you here that early?"

"She said she had promised to meet a potential buyer for one of her properties but that she had something else to do first."

"Did that person ever show up?"

"That's the funny part … no one did."

Bishop thought that it was more than odd. It seemed downright suspicious. Could Ms. Littleford have ordered Kelli in early that day so that Amy would be alone on her jog? Was it possible that that old lady had dispatched Amy herself, or had she conspired with someone else to do her bidding? Bishop remembered Amy's comments about Martha Littleford being more of a pit than a peach. There was clearly no love lost between them. He definitely would be back to meet this woman.

Just as Bishop was about to leave, Kelli's thoughts returned to her friend. "It's such a tragedy … a double tragedy."

"What do you mean 'double'?"

She looked at him as she grabbed another tissue. "She was two months pregnant."

***

81

Trying to contain his own emotions, he asked Kelli a few more questions. Amy had told her only a few days earlier. Kelli didn't know who the father was. Since Amy didn't offer that information, Kelli was reluctant to ask. She implied that Amy might not have been certain herself.

Before he left the office, he gave her his cell phone number hoping that she might remember something later that might be important. Back on the crowded sidewalk, he had a lot to ponder. Why hadn't Officer Minnehan mentioned the fact that Amy was pregnant? It certainly must have been in the coroner's report. The media might have presented her "accidental" death as an even greater tragedy if that had been included. Was there an attempt to keep that knowledge from the press? If so, who was behind it? Why would anyone want to suppress it?

After forty-plus years as an educator, Bishop couldn't really say that he was surprised by Kelli's revelation. Amy's personal life was her own business. She had been voted May Queen in high school, the young woman who best epitomized the values of Mary, the mother of God. He knew that people change, and people make mistakes. He was not about to make any personal judgments. He was convinced that Amy had been murdered, and this added information made him even more determined to find the culprit by the end of the week. What kind of person would commit such a horrific crime? And what possible reason could there be to take Amy's life and that of her unborn child?

Amy had felt comfortable enough with Kelli to tell her of her pregnancy. Whom else might she have told? Her boyfriend? Boyfriends? Might this individual have sought to evade his responsibility by taking her life and framing someone else by planting the Tilley hat at the scene of the crime? He had gone to the realty office hoping to get a few answers from Martha Littleford. Instead, he had more questions. The case was taking a darker turn.

***

Ignoring the sun beating down on his uncovered head, he wanted to make one more stop before meeting Ron for lunch. Traffic was moving slowly. A few vile-smelling construction vehicles rumbled through town. More people were on the sidewalks now. He wondered if they pegged him as a tourist or a local. He hoped for the latter. The likely reality was that they didn't really pay much attention to him at all. Families were squeezing in some final days of summer fun before the kids headed back to school. He passed a group of elderly tourists disembarking for lunch at a popular restaurant on Main Street. There were some scantily clad teenage girls walking toward him, laughing and talking and checking their phones. He wasn't sure that they saw him, and he was preparing to dart into the street to avoid bumping into them. At the very last minute, the phalanx broke, and he walked on.

He wanted to stop in at the Belvedere Inn and extend his condolences to Amy's co-workers. He was hoping that someone might know something, however seemingly insignificant it might seem to them. When he walked into the lobby, he was mildly surprised to find no one there, and no one was at the registration area either. As directed by a sign on the counter, he rang the call bell that was placed there. After hitting the button, he held the bell to stifle the jarring ring. A plain woman wearing a light gray pant suit quickly emerged from a back room. The bangs of her light brown hair came down to her eyebrows. She had several bracelets on one wrist. A large watch dominated the other. She had several gaudy rings on her fingers but no wedding ring.

"May I help you?" she asked pleasantly.

Bishop briefly explained who he was and that Amy Walsh, his former student, had helped arrange accommodations for him just a couple of days earlier. He added that much to his dismay, he had been the one who discovered her body. He felt like the old man in the poem, "The Rime of the Ancient Mariner," by Samuel Taylor Coleridge who repeatedly must confess his sin as part of his punishment. The difference was that Bishop hadn't committed any crime.

She listened carefully as he spoke, her facial expression turning more somber as he told his story. "I'm so sorry," she said earnestly. "That must have been quite a shock."

He nodded his agreement. "I'd like to extend my condolences to you and all of her co-workers here at the inn."

"That's very kind of you." She paused, then asked, "I'm sorry. What was your name again?"

"Bishop. Michael Bishop," he replied as he extended his hand. "And you are …?"

"Carole Perrault."

Bishop repeated the name to himself several times. He didn't want to forget it, but he didn't want to write it down as if she were being interrogated, although that was his plan. His memory lapses might be explained by his advancing age; however, he was surprised that she had to ask him to repeat his name. One of the hallmarks of excellent customer service is the ability to make that personal connection.

"Carole, you must be devastated by her death. How long have you been working here?"

"About a year and a half."

"I see. Would you say that you were close friends?"

Bishop could sense that Carole was beginning to feel uncomfortable about his questioning. He decided to share with her his belief that Amy's death wasn't an accident as most people assumed and that he hoped to find out who was responsible for what happened to her that day.

"You mean you think someone murdered her?" she asked with a mixture of shock and curiosity.

"Yes, I do. I'm hoping that someone will remember something that will lead me to the person who did this."

"Well, I didn't really know her that well," she said somewhat defensively. "I mean she is … or was … the manager, and I was the assistant manager so we rarely worked at the same time. We jogged together occasionally. Amy was really into fitness."

"That must be hard on you right now. Do you know when someone will take her place?"

"I'm the new manager," she said sheepishly.

"Oh! Congratulations!"

"Thanks," she answered. "I could use the bump in pay."

Bishop said nothing. He wondered how desperately she needed that raise. Could she have been desperate enough to push her friend to her death? That might explain the lack of a struggle at the scene. Amy would not have felt threatened if she encountered Carole on the footpath.

"Well, I should be letting you get back to work. Perhaps I'll see you at the services for Amy."

"I heard that Amy requested that there be no calling hours. The family is arranging a private funeral back in her home town."

"Oh, I just assumed …" He thanked her for her time and headed across the lobby to the exit. Halfway there, he turned around. Carole was still at the counter. "I forgot. I have one more question, if you don't mind."

"Sure," she responded, but her tone of voice was less enthusiastic.

"When I was here on Sunday night, Amy had a brief phone conversation with a guy … David, I believe … and it sounded as if she had just fired him."

"Yeah, that would be Dave Conway. She fired him, all right. That's another reason we're shorthanded here."

He looked directly at Carole and asked, "Do you think he would be capable of violence?"

She took full advantage of the way the question had been phrased. "Dave is different, if you know what I mean. I'm kinda glad he's out of here. He gave me the creeps sometimes."

"Did he ever threaten anyone that you know of?"

"No, but he did ask me out a few times."

Bishop said nothing, assuming that there was more to the story. There was.

"As a matter of fact, Amy actually went out with him for a while, but then she dumped him."

"Why would Amy have agreed to date a guy like that?"

Carole shrugged her shoulders. "Low standards, I guess. Well, I shouldn't speak ill of the dead. At least she never dated Kiki Cavendish," she added in her defense. "We bumped into him jogging on the Marginal Way last week, and she put him down so bad. I thought it was kinda funny."

Bishop wondered if Carole was exaggerating the encounter for some reason. Kiki wasn't exactly a heartthrob, but he did seem to be a decent person. He thanked her again, gave her his cell phone number in case she thought of anything else, and left the lobby. His short conversation had yielded three additional persons of interest. It seemed clear to him that Amy and Carole did not enjoy a close relationship. Might Carole have been envious of her more attractive boss? Might she have coveted the manager's job enough to get it by devious means? And then there was David. She seemed very willing to cast him in a poor light. Rejected as a boyfriend and then fired from his job, might he have sought to extract his measure of revenge? And what about mild-mannered and pet-loving Kiki? Of course, Bishop had initially met him at Hannaford's at the assumed time of Amy's death.

He started walking toward Bessie's Restaurant. He was hoping to relax a little bit, but he knew that the time for real relaxation would come only when the mystery of the death of Amy Walsh and her unborn baby had been resolved. Some other questions occurred to him. Why hadn't Carole mentioned that Amy was pregnant? Was that proof that the two weren't close, or did Carole have a reason to keep that information from him?

Chapter Nine

With Max settled in on the braided rug in the front porch, Ron left for the short walk to meet Bishop for lunch at Bessie's. He wanted to get there well before his friend so that he could arrange with the waitress to give him the check regardless of what his companion might say.

For a weekday, there was a decent crowd, but no queue of people waiting to be seated. A young woman with dark hair pulled back in a ponytail greeted him with her heavy accent.

"Gud afternoon, sir," she said brightly. "Wan for lunch?"

He waved two fingers at her as if he wasn't convinced that she would understand him. Then, he quickly realized that his assumption was foolish and said, "Two, please. I'm meeting a friend here."

"Pleese follow me," she said as she grabbed silverware, placemats, and menus. As he settled in, she said, "My name is Orjana. Can I get you drink while you wait for your fren?"

"I'll have a Coke, please."

"Sure things. I'll be bak in a minutes."

She had begun to make her way to get his drink when he called her back. He had completely forgotten her name. "Oh, miss?"

She turned back to him and smiled. "My name is Orjana. What can I do for you?"

Orjana. How could he forget such a beautiful name? "Orjana, would you please make sure to give me the check when we're done?"

"Of courz," she said with a conspiratorial grin. "I weel give you check no madder what she sayz."

"Thank you." Jennings didn't bother to correct Orjana's assumption that he was meeting a woman for lunch.

It was five minutes after one, and there was no sign of Bishop. Ron began to wonder if he had gotten the time wrong. In a moment of panic, he began to doubt if he was even at the right restaurant. Just then, Bishop walked in, sat down at the booth across from his friend, and apologized for being late.

"Glad you could make it," Ron said, taking advantage of the opportunity of teasing his good friend. "Here," he added as he passed a plastic bag across the table.

"What's this?" Bishop had completely forgotten that he had asked Ron to look around the shops for a replacement for his Tilley. He took one look at the cap. "Red Sox?" he said in mock disbelief. "Do you really expect me to wear this?"

"It's only for a few days, and besides, I didn't think you'd want to waste time driving down to Kittery just to see if they had a Tilley."

Bishop put the hat on, took it off to adjust the band, and put it back on again. "Do I look like a real New Englander now?"

When the waitress noticed that Ron's friend had arrived, she went over to their booth.

"Orjana! How nice to see you again!" She smiled in recognition of the man who not only had correctly identified her accent, but also had left a generous tip and remembered her name.

90

"You know my name. What is yours, pleese?"

"Michael Bishop," he said as he extended his hand. "And this is Ron Jennings, the assistant principal at the school where I teach."

"Nice to meet you both. What would you like for drink?"

"I'll have water with lemon, please."

"And you, Meester Yehnings. Would you like another Coke?"

Jennings, intrigued by her accent, looked at his almost empty glass. "Yes, thank you."

"I weel be bak in a minutes to take your order." On her way to get the drinks, she stopped to pick up some empty plates from another table.

"Is that a Russian accent?"

"Slovenian."

"I wonder how she ended up in Ogunquit." Orjana might have asked the same question of each man.

It didn't take either one long to decide what to have for lunch. After closing the menus, Bishop began to question Ron on what, if anything, he had picked up other than the hat. He spoke in a hushed tone. "What are folks on the street saying about Amy's death?"

Ron was somewhat embarrassed to report that he hadn't picked up much of anything. Some people hadn't heard about it, and others simply dismissed it as an accident.

Before Bishop could respond, Orjana returned to take their order.

"What can I get for you guys?"

Ron, who was by this time, famished, went first. "I'll have a BLT and an order of onion rings."

"Very gud. And for you, Meester Beeshop?"

"I'll have a cup of fish chowdah and a lobstah roll."

As Orjana glided off to put in their orders, Ron was laughing. "Sounds like you've picked up that Boston accent pretty fast."

"It's this hat," he deadpanned as he removed it and placed it by his side.

Ron already had his eye on the assortment of desserts prominently displayed in a glass case that most patrons would have to walk by. "I hope your morning was more productive than mine."

Just as Bishop was about to respond, Ron's cell vibrated. He glanced at the screen. "It's a text from Terry."

Knowing how much the actions of Sister Ann since her return bothered the assistant principal, he told him that he might as well look at it now and get it over with.

Ron read the message and began tapping rapidly on his screen. After a short pause, he received a reply to which he quickly responded again. The exchanges continued for a couple of minutes. Then, he put the phone down.

"Well?" Bishop surmised that the texts had something to do with the White family's visit to the school.

Ron's slumped shoulders and glum facial expression were indicative of just how bad it was. "Terry checked with Sarah in

Guidance, and sure enough, Sarah was told to make out a schedule for Jeff on the spot."

"You sort of expected that, anyway. Maybe the kid deserves another chance."

"I really don't believe that he does, or I would have given him one myself. But it gets worse."

Orjana arrived and began placing the hot food in front of them. "Pleese enjoy. I will chain you to your seets unteel you eet every bite," she added with a straight face. Ron gave her a quizzical look, but Bishop who had heard this line before, simply smiled.

Ron popped a whole onion ring in his mouth before realizing just how hot it was. He waved his hand furiously in front of his mouth and gulped some of his Coke. Once he could talk, he explained what else he had learned.

"Apparently, Terry has welcomed the new business manager, Christine Webster, into her close circle of confidants."

"Gossips," Bishop corrected as he savored the chowder.

"Whatever. At any rate, Chris told Terry that Sister Ann had given her a check to deposit. Guess who wrote the check?"

"Mr. White, I would imagine."

"Yup! And for how much?"

"Probably tuition for the year?"

"That's about seven grand, isn't it?"

Bishop nodded his agreement.

"According to Chris, the check was for twenty-five thousand dollars. When she gave the check to Chris, she said, 'Enter this in as a donation.'"

"Very generous of the White family," Bishop commented sarcastically.

"There's more," warned Ron. Bishop simply raised his eyebrows in anticipation. "As she was leaving the office, Sister Ann told Chris, 'And don't forget to bill them for full tuition and fees.'"

Bishop swallowed, wiped his mouth, and said as much to himself as to Ron, "I don't believe this!" Clearly, the implication was that he *did* believe it. A little extortion to start her day? He hoped that Sister Ann might have changed as a result of her suspension. She had. She was emboldened. He briefly considered informing Sister Estelle, assuming he could conceal his sources. The problem was that Estelle might be pleased with the principal's ability to get big donors to support the school. Having wrangled her way back into her job, Ann was acting without fear of repercussion. Two questions occurred to Bishop. First, how did Sister Ann convince Sister Estelle to end her suspension with no further disciplinary action? Second, who would be able to stop her this time?

***

The two men spent a few moments quietly working on their lunch. Ron finished first, as was usually the case when they ate together. Still fuming over Terry's texts, he wanted to talk about something else. "How's that lobster … I mean *lobstah* … roll?"

"Delicious. Even the best seafood in Groveland doesn't taste like this. You should try one before we leave."

"I'm planning on it," Ron admitted. Ron had to be the only person Bishop knew who began planning future meals immediately after eating.

When Orjana returned to take their plates, she said impishly, "I'm glad that you eet every bite on you plates so I don't have to chain you to your seets." Ron still hadn't quite figured out what to make of the waitress.

"Can I intrest you in someting else, guys?"

Ron, who had been eyeing the desserts, didn't need much prodding. "What desserts do you have today?"

Orjana rattled off mouth-watering descriptions of seven or eight pies without referring to any notes. As if Ron needed convincing, she added, "They're reelly good."

Without much hesitation, Ron announced his selection. "Banana Meringue, please."

She turned to Bishop. "I'll try the Boston Cream."

"It must be that hat," Ron said as he laughed.

Orjana quickly returned with two of the largest slices of pie that either man had ever seen. Bishop smiled at Orjana. "Please don't chain me to my seat if I don't clean this plate."

"No, no," she said through her laughter. "That duz not apply to dessert."

Once they dug in, Ron asked Bishop about his morning.

"I checked in with Officer Minnehan, and it was as if he had forgotten that he considered me a person of interest and had told me not to leave town. He told me that the coroner ruled Amy's death an accident, and that ended that. He even offered to return my hat to me, but I didn't want it. As a matter of fact, I'm glad you didn't find a Tilley. Too many bad memories."

Ron listened as he tackled his pie. Bishop had taken a few bites of his pie as he recounted his morning. He knew that he would need a box to take the leftovers back to the cottage.

"I just don't understand why everyone now seems content to view this as an accident. The positioning of the body and the planting of the hat nearby suggest something more sinister. Why cover it up? And I got the impression that Minnehan knew more than he was willing to say."

"I suppose a murder would be bad for business," Ron offered as the pie on his plate rapidly diminished in size.

Bishop gave Jennings a look. Of course! Why he hadn't he thought of that? "You're absolutely right! News of a young woman murdered on the Marginal Way would be devastating to a town where tourism is the name of the game."

"Do you need a box for that pie, Meester Beeshop?"

"Yes, please, and the check."

Bishop told Ron that he would fill him in on the rest of his morning on the walk home. Orjana returned and handed the box to Bishop. He reached out for the check, but Orjana pulled her hand back and make a dramatic delivery of the check to Ron who winked his approval.

"I see I've been out-maneuvered this time," he said with a smile. He hoped that he wouldn't be so easily out-maneuvered by Amy's killer.

Ron signed the credit card receipt as both men prepared to leave. Just as they reached the door, Orjana called out. "Meester Beeshop! You forgot your hat!"

He turned back to see Orjana, Red Sox cap in hand, rush towards him.

"Thank you so much! I guess I'd forget my head if it wasn't attached," he said laughing.

Orjana smiled as she worked through that idiom. Bishop decided not to embarrass her by trying to explain it to her. He simply had to be more aware of some limitations in her command of English. However, she had a much better command of English than he did of Slovenian or any other foreign language.

"I like your udder hat more bedder," she added sweetly.

Now, it was Bishop's turn to be confused. "My other hat?"

"Ya, the one you had on for deener the udder night."

Was it possible that he had left his Tilley here? He had called to see if anyone had turned it in, but no one knew anything about it. "Do you remember what it looked like?"

"Oh sure," she said as she made a big circle around her head. "It had a beeg … how you say … brim?"

"Do you remember seeing me leave with that hat on my head?"

"No, sorry. I was beezy."

"Well, Orjana, thanks again. You've been very helpful. We'll be back."

Once they left the restaurant, a warm blast of air hit them. It took a couple of minutes to adjust to the change in temperature.

Instead of walking back to the cottage, they decided to take a walk on the beach. They crossed Shore Road and headed down Beach Street. Bishop put his new cap on and said to Ron, "I hope you left Orjana a very good tip."

"I did. She's a delightful young girl."

Bishop nodded his agreement. "I must have just grabbed my jacket and left the hat on the shelf."

"At least you know that much."

Bishop stopped walking and looked at this friend. "I know more than that."

"What do you mean?"

"Whoever took my hat from that shelf killed Amy."

Chapter Ten

Once they got to the clean, warm sand, they took off their shoes, left them there, and walked out on the muddy, flat ocean floor. They were only about a tenth of a mile from the restaurant, but the cool breeze coming off of the water dropped the real feel temperature considerably. Some families had set up umbrellas on the beach. Children were too busy making mud castles to notice these two men going by. They encountered some folks walking the opposite way. Most made eye contact and smiled; a few averted their gaze. One guy wearing a pair of swimming trunks that came down to his knees noticed Bishop's hat, asked, "How'd the Sox do last night?"

Bishop had gone to bed before the game ended. Ron answered, "They won, 3 – 1. Big Papi's homer was the difference." The man, whose belly hung over the waistband of his trunks, gave up a "thumbs up" as he walked on.

After walking at a fairly good clip, Bishop walked into the frigid water about ankle deep and gazed out as the waves broke and rolled relentlessly towards shore and dissolution. Internally, he was still preoccupied by the events of that morning. He already shared with Ron what had transpired in the police station when he checked in with Minnehan. As they stood there, some sandpipers were patrolling the water's edge, their legs moving rapidly as they walked from one destination to another.

Ron listened as Bishop recounted his conversations with Kelli in the office of Littleford Realty and with Carole, the new manager of the Belvedere Inn. He picked up some flat stones and skipped them across the water. One of them skipped nine times before it dipped down out of sight. When the older man finished his summary, he picked up a perfectly shaped stone that skipped seventeen times as it arced to the right.

"Impressive!" commented Ron.

"The stone skipping or the information?"

"Both. I hate to say it, but it sounds as though both that old lady Littleford and Carole had some reason to want Amy out of the way."

"I wouldn't discount the possibility of Kelli Dempsey casting her boss in a negative light to deflect attention from herself. I'll know more when I have a chance to meet with Littleford."

"Don't forget about that David character that Amy dated. He might not have taken too kindly to being dumped."

"Or perhaps to being informed that he was about to become a father," added Bishop ominously. "He's on my list."

"And what about that guy that you encountered at the footbridge where Amy died. He certainly acted in a strange manner."

Both men started to walk back to pick up their shoes. "He could be totally extraneous to the case. On the other hand," he added soberly, "it might turn out that he and David are one and the same."

It was a possibility that Ron hadn't even considered.

***

As Bishop unlocked the door, he heard Max scrambling to greet him. Ron volunteered to take the dog for a walk. Bishop appreciated the offer as he was physically exhausted. He headed for the comfortable chaise in the front porch hoping to catch a nap. Since the tide was out, the soothing sounds of the surf were only faintly discernible. He definitely missed his daily dose of classical music. Then he remembered that there was a clock radio on the small table beside his bed. Sitting on the bed, he searched for a classical station. He stopped at each station with a strong signal only long enough to determine its content. He caught snippets of commercials for laundry detergent promising to get your clothes "whiter than white" whatever that meant, and a car dealership specializing in financing for those "with bad credit" which didn't appear to be a sound business plan to him. Moving the dial, he heard The Supremes singing, "Stop! In the Name of Love," which he ignored, and then one of Ron's favorites, Willie Nelson's "Always on My Mind."

Just as he decided that the state of Maine lacked a classical music station, he tuned in to 106.9 FM. The announcer on WBACH introduced the next selection titled *Three Graces* composed by Carolyn Yarnell. He listened intently to music that he had never heard before and turned the radio off as soon as the piece concluded. The sounds lingered as he closed his eyes and thought of the Three Graces of Greek mythology, Charm, Beauty, and Creativity. He thought of *his* Grace who embodied all of those qualities. He fell asleep dreaming that he and Grace were walking the beach, hand in hand once again.

***

Bishop didn't even realize that Ron had returned until Max woke him up by jumping on the bed. After reminding his animal friend that furniture, especially furniture that he did not own, was off limits, he found Ron in the kitchen, snacking on a bag of chips, and talking on the phone. He waved a greeting, went into the living room, and flipped on the television. Cable service provided a number of channels, but after a few minutes of surfing, he gave up.

On either side of the large screen TV, there were built-in shelves with a number of mostly glass items with a nautical theme. There were also some books that he decided to examine more closely. Among them was a copy of *The Scarlet Letter* by Nathaniel Hawthorne. That novel, considered by many to be one of the three great American novels, was like an old friend to the man who had been teaching English for well over forty years. In fact, he had assigned this novel to his incoming seniors as one of their summer assignments. At least he hoped that they were all reading it and not just some study guide. He carefully removed that volume from the stack, but as he did, several smaller volumes slid, like dominoes, against the retreating bookend. One red leather-bound book with its top and bottom pages beautifully gilded caught his attention.

It was a first edition of *The Collected Poetry of Celia Thaxter*. Years ago, Bishop and Grace had taken a boat ride from Portsmouth, New Hampshire out to the Isles of Shoals, nine miles from the coast. Thaxter, a minor poet and writer of the 19th century, lived on Appledore Island with her father who was a lighthouse keeper. Living in that relative isolation, she became a keen observer of the beauty of nature and its effects on her. Bishop and his young wife had strolled the grounds and gardens just as Thaxter had done.

He recalled that her residence had become a mecca for more famous writers such as James Russell Lowell, Henry Wadsworth Longfellow, and even Hawthorne himself.

He opened the volume to a page that had been marked by a thin gold ribbon. He scanned the page and read this line: *One golden day redeems a weary year.* He sat on the sofa and read some of her other observations. That one line kept coming back to him. In many ways, the last year had been a trying one for the veteran teacher. The students were not the problem; the administration was. He had even considered retiring at one point. When Sister Ann and Sister Pat, a.k.a. Mayhem and Meany, were suspended weeks before the end of the school year, he thought that that "golden day" had arrived. The unexpected return of Sister Ann put an end to those hopes. And even though he had only been in Ogunquit for a few days, it also felt like "a weary year." He knew that the only chance he had for a "golden day" was to figure out who killed Amy Walsh. To compound his problem, he had only a few more days to do just that.

***

Ron came in asking, "Any ideas about dinner?"

Bishop put the book down. He expected to have this conversation every evening. "There are some burgers and hot dogs in the fridge. I thought we'd keep it simple tonight."

"Fine with me."

"Mind if I ask who was on the phone?"

"Mary Ellen. I gave her a brief rundown of what's been going on here. She's upset that she couldn't be here to help catch the

103

guy who did it, but she's got all she can handle with her accounting class."

"That's interesting," Bishop said.

"What's interesting?"

"That she assumed the culprit is a man."

"I hadn't thought of that. Of course, she may not have meant that literally."

"Of course." He thought of all of the people who might have had a reason to do Amy harm: Martha Littleford, Kelli, Carole, David, the man at the footbridge, and the baby's father. It seemed an even split of men and women at this point.

"She sends her love by the way," Ron added. "I'll get the grill going."

With the prospect of food in the offing, Max followed Ron outside.

Bishop put a couple of plates on the dining room table, and grabbed a container of potato salad and a couple of beers from the fridge. Not long afterward, Ron brought in a steaming platter of burgers, hot dogs, and warm slices of the French bread he bought that morning.

"Have any condiments?" Ron asked as he was about to dig in.

Bishop slapped his forehead. "Sorry. I guess I didn't think of everything."

"Just a sec," Ron said as he rushed out to his car. A minute later, he came back with his hands full of packets of ketchup, mustard, salt, and pepper. "Sometimes, I get extras at the drive-thru," he said sheepishly.

Maybe it was the sea air, but both men were famished. After the main course, Bishop had the rest of his Boston cream pie, and Ron had one of the chocolate éclairs.

"I'll bet Mary Ellen doesn't know that you're a grill master."

"And let's keep it that way," he said laughing but meaning every word.

***

Ron settled on the sofa to watch the Red Sox take on the Indians again. On the coffee table nearby, he had a peanut butter and jelly sandwich, some pretzels, and a Coke to fortify himself through the first few innings. Bishop told him that he could have the second éclair, but he declined, at least for the moment.

After taking Max for a long walk around the neighborhood, Bishop sat in the darkened porch watching flashes of heat lightning in the distance. He couldn't help but think of Hester Prynne, the young woman in Hawthorne's novel whose illegitimate child brought her such joy but also a world of pain. His psychological masterpiece taught some invaluable lessons. Each of the major characters withheld key information. Prynne withheld the name of the father in an attempt to protect him. The Reverend Arthur Dimmesdale refused to admit that he was the father in attempt to avoid the public shame. Roger Chillingworth withheld that fact he was Hester's husband from the townspeople in order to torture Dimmesdale whom he had correctly surmised to be the father. Each of these decisions resulted in a greater tragedy. Bishop could only wonder what secrets were hidden here in Ogunquit. Had Amy told the father of her pregnancy? What was the source of tension between Amy and Martha Littleford? Was Kelli's explanation of why she didn't join Amy on her run that morning the real reason? Why did Minnehan quickly switch his belief that Bishop's hat made him a person of interest? Why did the media dismiss Amy's death as an accident? Who was the man Bishop startled at the footbridge? What had he placed in his pocket? Did David decide to take revenge against Amy after she fired him? How far might Carole have been willing to go to take Amy's place as the manager of the inn?

He had some theories, but they were just that ... theories. He had only a few more days to find those answers, but he wasn't even certain that he was asking the right questions. Someone knew something that would break the case open. And even if someone wasn't intentionally concealing something, someone might be in possession of some critical clue and not be aware of it. Just then, he heard the first rumbles of thunder in the distance.

Chapter Eleven

The next morning, it was Bishop who woke to an empty house, empty that is except for Max who was more than ready to begin his new morning ritual. As far as he was concerned, Ogunquit was their new home. When Bishop went into the kitchen, he found a note from Ron. *Just stepped out to pick up a few things. Max has been walked. Don't let his sad brown eyes fool you. He's been fed too.*

He crumpled the note and tossed it in the garbage container under the sink. Minutes later, he heard Ron's Nissan pulling into the driveway. Despite slipping on the smooth kitchen floor to gain traction, Max made a mad dash to the door. Ron had been on a bit of a shopping spree. He had a couple of plastic bags full of miscellaneous items. In addition, he had a cardboard carton from Dunkin' Donuts with two large steaming cups of coffee. Also, he had managed to grab a copy of *The Weekly Sentinel* that the artist Bishop had met on the Marginal Way told him came out every Wednesday.

The two men quickly put the groceries away and sat down to enjoy a morning coffee. Ron opened a smaller bag that contained some fresh bagels wrapped in waxed paper and took a container of cream cheese from the fridge. Bishop took one bite of a poppy seed bagel. "Delicious! Where did you get these?"

"You mentioned Hannaford's, so I went there," he replied as he loaded more cream cheese onto his cinnamon raisin bagel. "I think I saw that guy that helped you track down Max that day."

"You mean Kiki?"

"Yeah. He was restocking some shelves so I didn't see his name tag, but he had red hair and a bunch of tattoos on his arms and neck."

"Sounds like him," Bishop concluded. The mention of Kiki's name brought back memories of discovering Amy's body, the bee sting that landed him in the hospital, and the interrogation by Officer Minnehan.

He went upstairs to get his reading glasses, came back down, and began flipping through the newspaper. After a couple of minutes, he said, "Hm. This is interesting."

"What is?" asked Bishop politely, expecting that Ron had found some sports story that he felt compelled to share.

He read the item word for word. "Kaye Whitehead, Commissioner of the Board of Elections for the Town of Ogunquit announced that the name of Amy S. Walsh (D) will remain on the ballot in the race for a seat on the Board of Selectmen this fall. The deadline for filing a petition to appear on the ballot has passed, she explained, and the ballot cannot be changed. Ms. Walsh, who died unexpectedly, was making her first run for office against incumbent Miriam L. Gladstone (R)."

"May I see that, please?" Bishop felt a jolt of adrenaline. He wasn't sure if it was the coffee or the unexpected bit of information. He read the brief story that Ron had just finished reading to him. Then he scanned the paper looking for any other reference to Amy. There was none.

"I didn't realize that Amy was running for office," Ron said.

"Neither did I," Bishop admitted. "I wonder why none of the folks I've talked to even mentioned it."

Ron thought for a moment, took a sip of coffee, and said, "I guess they felt that it didn't really matter anymore."

"Well, it matters to one person at a minimum."

With a puzzled look, he asked, "Who's that?"

"Miriam L. Gladstone."

"She probably would have won anyway, don't you think?"

Now, it was Bishop's turn to look puzzled. "Why would you say that?"

"This Gladstone lady is an incumbent, and incumbents usually win." Bishop simply frowned, suggesting that he wasn't willing to accept that that had to be true in this case. "And she's a Republican. In a small wealthy resort town like this, that's probably a huge advantage."

Bishop couldn't argue that point. He decided, however, that he wanted to know more about Ms. Gladstone and why Amy was running against her. Politics, he knew, could be a dirty business. She might have felt threatened by Amy's candidacy. How far might she have gone to eliminate that threat?

***

Bishop knew that most of the bits and pieces of information that he had gathered were probably of no consequence. He was also cognizant of the fact the one piece of information that would break open the case might already be in his possession, but that he just hadn't made the connection yet. If he were home, he would have hopped on his riding mower for a few hours, knowing that as he performed that mindless chore, his mind was somehow at work on the problem at hand. With no lawn to mow, and with the beach just minutes away, he decided to take a long walk alone.

Sister Ann had begun flooding Ron's email with questions about rather inconsequential matters. He was grateful that she hadn't called or texted, at least not yet, but he was somewhat annoyed that he couldn't take a few days of vacation uninterrupted. Apparently, it was just one more way that the principal was reminding him that she was back, and he worked for her. While Bishop headed out for his walk on this sunny late August day, Ron decided to stay put for a few hours and respond as best he could to all of her messages.

Dressed in tan khaki shorts, a light blue golf shirt, and his new cap, Bishop walked at a decent pace. His intention was to go about two miles down the beach to the famous footbridge which residents on that side of town used at high tide to cross over the Ogunquit River to gain access to the beach. It was hard to overstate the pleasure that the scenic beauty of that place brought to him, but the serenity of Ogunquit had been marred by an evil act. Why was he pursuing the truth regarding Amy's demise and not the police? With the wind at his back, he returned to the center of town to ask Officer Minnehan that very question.

***

Ron was annoyed as he worked his way through Sister Ann's emails. Most could have been dealt with by simply asking the Terry in the main office, Sarah in the guidance office, or someone else on the staff. *Where is the list of locker combinations? Did Mr. Cahill have any special setup requests for his talk on Conference Day? Do you know why Andy Steinberg didn't show up for summer football practice?* The list went on. He did note, however, that she made no comment on the job that he had done as interim principal while she was suspended. The only good news was that, despite bombarding him with trivial questions, she had not asked him to return home early. At least, she hadn't asked yet.

Bishop was still out when he finished his replies, and since it was nearing lunchtime, and food was never very far from his thoughts, he began to search the Internet for a good place to have lunch. It didn't take him long to find a number of intriguing choices. As he jotted down a few notes, his cell rang. He thought it might be Mary Ellen or perhaps Bishop and said a quick prayer that it wasn't Sister Ann. When he looked at the screen, he realized that it was Terry.

"Hey, Terr, what's up?"

"How's the weather up there?"

"It's been perfect so far."

"How's Michael doing?"

"Okay, I guess. He's obsessed with the idea that that woman was killed, and frankly, there seem to be a few people that might have wanted her out of the way."

"Well, if anyone can get to the truth, it's Michael. He's relentless, and he doesn't miss a single thing."

"The problem is that we have to leave on Saturday."

"You may want to stay there a little longer ... like forever," she said, unable to hide her frustration.

"Why? What's wrong? Are you in the office right now?"

"No. Sarah's watching the desk for me. I'm around outside trying to cool off in this heat."

"Terry, that doesn't make any sense," he said gently.

"It will when you hear what happened."

He had no idea what to expect. "I'm listening."

Terry took a deep breath and then began to tell her story. "I was sitting at my desk working on some boring forms that Sister Ann asked me to complete. There aren't many people around here this week, and with the A/C humming along, I was lost in my own little world. "Suddenly," she said as she raised her voice dramatically, "I hear this strange tapping on one of the windows to my right. I thought it might be a bird or something."

Ron waited for her to continue the story. Had she forgotten to close all of the windows? Had a bird or squirrel gotten into the office? It couldn't be that bad, he thought as he waited for her to continue.

"I look over and this woman in a motorized scooter is hitting the window with a cane. I thought I was gonna have a heart attack then and there. Once she had my attention, she started yelling. 'Am I going to have to sit out here all day? Open the damn door, why don'tcha?"

"Maybe I got up too fast cause I felt a little dizzy, but I managed to open the door."

"Did you know this person?"

"Oh, yeah! You know her, too!" Terry liked to extend the drama when she had a good story to tell. Ron couldn't think of anyone he knew who used a scooter.

"Well, who is it?" he asked impatiently.

"Sister Patricia Meehan." There was a moment of stunned silence as Ron began to feel a bit disoriented himself.

"Sister Pat?"

"The one and only … Sister Meany."

"But Sister Estelle sent her to work at a soup kitchen far away from Groveland and far away from Sister Ann," he remarked as if reviewing those facts would make Sister Pat disappear.

"That's ancient history now. I was speechless, which as you know, doesn't happen very often. As she scooted in the open door, I managed to ask her what she did to her foot which is in a cast up to her knee."

Sister Pat enjoyed talking about herself almost as much as she enjoyed badmouthing others. Terry summarized her story for Ron. Apparently, Sister was working in the kitchen as usual. She tried to grab a supersized can of tomato sauce from a shelf, and it slipped out of her hands and landed on her right foot.

"And she's in a scooter because of that? Wouldn't that probably just cause a bruise?"

Terry laughed and continued to explain that the can falling on her foot might have resulted in just a bruise, but Sister Pat reacted to the pain by hopping around on her left foot until she slipped on a wet spot, fell and broke that foot in three places. She ended up in surgery and had a couple of pins inserted to stabilize her foot. Terry added that Sister would be in that cast for a couple of months and then would need additional time for therapy.

Ron smiled as he tried to visualize his colleague hopping on one foot. Given her girth, she barely managed to get around on two feet. He imagined that the scooter was being taxed to the limit. Then he got serious again and asked Terry the obvious question. "What is she doing at Holy Trinity? Visiting?"

"Wishful thinking, pal. There was no one to take care of her up there, so they sent her back here to recuperate."

"But that will take months?" Ron couldn't believe what was happening. "Is she going to resume her role as assistant principal … of whatever?"

"Don't know yet, but I want to slap her already."

"Now, now, Terry … "

"After telling me her sad story, she steered her scooter right towards Sister Ann's office. You know what she said to me as she breezed by?"

Ron was afraid to ask, but he knew she would tell him anyway.

"She said, and I quote, 'Are you pregnant or something? You must have gained twenty pounds.' Can you imagine the nerve of that woman? She'd give the fat lady in the circus a run for her money." Terry was so upset that she practically spat out the words.

114

Ron tried to calm her down by changing the subject. He filled her in on the progress of Bishop's investigation such as it was. She expressed confidence in the English teacher's ability to get to the bottom of the mystery.

"You and I both know that he's done it before … several times, in fact. I know he loves teaching, but sometimes I think he missed his calling."

"I think he'd rather write a mystery than have to solve one, especially one involving a former student."

Terry promised to keep Ron informed of any new developments at school.

Not long after that, Bishop returned looking rather tired. He told his friend that after a long walk on the beach, he had decided to check in with Minnehan.

"You can tell me all about it in the car. I'm starving."

Chapter Twelve

"Where are we going?" Bishop asked as they got into Ron's car and rolled down all the windows.

"Maine Diner. It's on Route 1 in Wells, not too far from here."

"Can't say that I've heard of it." To Bishop, lunch was lunch, but to his friend, every meal was serious business.

"I did a little research online this morning, and this place is apparently a "must" if you're in the area. They've had a lot of national attention over the years. Apparently, it's one of Luis Tiant's favorite spots," he added enthusiastically. "You do know who he is, don't you?"

"El Tiante? Of course," he said breezily. "He's in the Red Sox Hall of Fame, if I'm not mistaken."

Ron laughed. "When did you become an expert on Sox history?"

"Must be the hat," deadpanned Bishop.

The restaurant might only be several miles away, but Route 1 was far from a speedway. With a fair amount of traffic and more than a fair amount of traffic lights, Ron turned on the radio to a rock station. Bishop didn't complain as the volume was down, and at least it wasn't the country music he usually listened to. He began to recount his second visit to the police station.

"The young African American woman who checked in all visitors didn't seem surprised to see me again."

"'Minnehan?'" she had asked perfunctorily. I soon found myself in the same very warm room sitting in the same uncomfortable chair. He came in, clearly annoyed by my return."

"'I told you that you were free to go.'"

"I looked him at him and fired back, 'Whoever killed the pregnant Amy Walsh is also still free.' He tried to look shocked, but Minnehan wasn't a very good actor. He scratched the back of his neck, trying to think of what to say. I told him that the autopsy report would have included the fact that Amy was pregnant. He tried to defend himself by saying that he didn't think that it was relevant, but I wasn't buying it."

At that point in the story, Ron slammed on the brakes as the car in front of them slowed to a stop for no apparent reason. Fortunately, he avoided a collision and passed along a few choice words to the other driver.

"Okay, you can get back to that story," he said sheepishly.

"At that point Minnehan suggested that we go for a walk. As we left the building, he told the receptionist that he'd be back in a few minutes. Once outside, he admitted that he knew that Amy was pregnant. I took a chance and said, 'And my guess is that you're the father.'"

Ron turned to look at his passenger in disbelief.

"If you don't mind, keep your eyes on the road. We just had one close call," he reminded him.

Ron admired his friend's bold technique of letting the person you're questioning assume that you know more than you actually do.

He had successfully used the same technique in questioning students more than once. He was more than curious as to whether or not it worked on Minnehan. "What did he say?"

"He asked me how I knew, and I replied, 'I didn't.' Then he told me that he had dated Amy on and off for a year, but that he knew there had been other guys."

"That might explain why he wanted to drop the investigation," Ron suggested.

"That's exactly what I said to him."

"How did react?"

"At first, he didn't say any ..." He stopped mid-sentence when they passed a sign indicating that they had just entered the town of Kennebunk. "I thought you said this place was in Wells."

"It is," Ron said as his face flushed and he slammed his hand on the steering wheel. "I must have missed it," he added as he looked for a place to turn around. Once they were back on the right track, they both began to pay more attention to their surroundings.

"Well, doesn't the fact that he admitted he's the father make him a suspect?"

"In theory, yes, but the more he talked about her, the more convinced I became that he had nothing to do with it. He even asked to marry her, but she said she wasn't ready for that kind of commitment." He thought back to the events of that Monday morning. "It must have been very difficult for him to have been one of the officers who arrived on the scene that day."

"Then why did he conclude that her death was an accident after initially accusing you of being involved?"

"He didn't. He was told not to pursue it."

Before he could begin to explain what Minnehan told him, he saw the blue and white building and the large sign for the Maine Diner. "We're here. This is it!"

Ron slowed abruptly and swung into the crowded parking lot. He cruised the first aisle looking for a spot and stalked a family of five walking to their vehicle. As they pulled away, he pulled right in. "That's always a good sign," he said as he turned off the engine and prepared to get out.

"What is? That you found a spot?"

"Well, that too, but this place is packed. That means good food."

The hostess, a young girl who looked a bit frazzled, told them that the wait was twenty to twenty-five minutes. Bishop would have been tempted to go elsewhere, but Ron had no problem with that. The aromas emanating from the kitchen only increased his hunger level from starving to famished.

Once they were called to be seated, Ron wasted little time looking at the menu that he had studied online.

"My name is Mark," said a tall young man with thick hair cut long on top and buzzed close to his head on the sides. "Can I start you gentlemen off with something to drink?"

"I'll have the Clam Cake Plate and a Coke, please." Bishop, who had just begun to study the menu, simply closed his. "Same for me."

"Hope I didn't rush you."

"No problem. I'm sure it'll be good."

As they waited for their order, Ron asked Bishop who ordered Minnehan not to press for an investigation.

"The chairman of the Friends of the Marginal Way. He told him that a murder investigation would ruin tourism. He didn't want any negative publicity with the big Labor Day weekend coming up. Local businesses would take a big hit and that would be bad for everyone, including Minnehan."

"Sounds like this guy was threatening to have him fired if he didn't play ball."

"Right."

"Did he give you the name of this chairman?"

"Ray Gladstone."

Ron strained to make the connection. "Sounds familiar."

"Yes, it does. Ray Gladstone is the husband of Miriam L. Gladstone, Amy's political opponent." After Mark delivered their meals, Bishop said in a hushed tone, "He's also the brother-in-law of Martha Littleford, someone who didn't get along very well with Amy."

As Ron dug into the huge platter of crab cakes before him, he said, "I wonder if those three had anything to do with Amy's death."

"I don't know," replied Bishop, "but I plan on finding out."

***

Ron waited for his friend to push his plate aside before he caught Mark's attention.

"Anything else I can get for you gentlemen?"

Gesturing to his unfinished lunch, Bishop laughed. "Not for me! That was very filling."

Ron, however, didn't hesitate to order. "I'll have the Maine Indulgence, please, with extra whipped cream and another Coke."

Since they were going to be there a while longer, Bishop decided to order a cup of tea. Ron's eyes widened as his dessert arrived. He proceeded to demolish the large waffle, topped with blueberry ice cream with chocolate chips, smothered in maple syrup and whipped cream. For the older man, that would have been an entire meal. He marveled at his friend's ability to eat whatever he wanted. Since he didn't spend much time exercising, he obviously was blessed with an active metabolism.

As they headed back to Ogunquit, Ron listened to the radio, and his passenger mulled over some possibilities. Was it possible that Ray Gladstone wanted to squelch publicity about Amy's death, not for fear of an adverse effect on tourism, but to deflect attention from his own role in her murder? Could Amy's challenge to his wife's reelection have led to her death? Why was the relationship between Amy and Martha so strained? In the phone conversation that Amy had with her that Sunday night, Amy acknowledged that Martha was upset but hoped she could leave the past in the past.

121

What was that all about? Could Martha have sought revenge on her own, or might she have been helped by her sister and brother-in-law?

"Guess what?" Ron suddenly blurted out.

"Guess Who," responded Bishop coming out of his reverie.

Ron hesitated to correct his friend, but he suspected that either he wasn't paying attention, or he was having some difficulty with his hearing.

"No, I said, 'Guess what?'"

"I know you did, but I'm pretty sure that's The Guess Who."

Ron smiled as he understood Bishop's game. He turned the radio up and began singing the lyrics to *No Time* by The Guess Who. For Bishop, it was a moment of comic relief, but it didn't last long. He realized that he had very little time left to find justice for Amy and her unborn child.

"Well, what were you going to tell me?" He thought it might have to do with the meal they just had or the one he was planning for tonight.

"I had a call this morning from Terry."

"What did Sister Ann do this time?" It still upset him to think about the fact that Sister Estelle had allowed her to return as the principal.

"It's not her. The other half of Mayhem and Meany is back!"

He removed his glasses and put his right hand over his eyes. He said softly, "Un … be … lievable. Did she get her old job back?" Sister Pat had been one of the two assistant principals until she was suspended along with her cohort. Exactly what her duties were was never very clear. She spent most of her time meddling, criticizing, and scheming.

"Terry wasn't sure about that, but it seemed as if Sister Ann was expecting her arrival. Pat was in a motorized scooter having broken her foot working at the soup kitchen."

The image of the rotund administrator sitting on one of those scooters made him smile. "Once she realized that Pat had returned, I wouldn't be surprised if she didn't inflict that injury on herself just to wrangle her way back in."

"You really think so?"

"Let's put it this way. Never underestimate what those two are capable of doing."

As they turned off Route 1, Bishop asked Ron if he would be willing to return to the cottage by himself and take care of Max. "Drop me off near Littleford Realty. There's someone there I need to talk to."

Chapter Thirteen

As they approached a stop sign, Bishop saw the queue of five or six cars ahead of them. "This is close enough," he said as he opened the passenger door. "I'll see you back at the cottage." Walking at a reasonable pace, he reached the intersection before Ron did. Before he got to the realtor's office, he pulled out his cell phone to put it on standby mode. He noticed that he had a message from someone in the 207 area code. That meant it was a local call. He must have missed it while having lunch. He decided to listen.

Hi, Mr. Bishop. This is Carole Perrault at the Belvedere. You asked me to give you a call if I thought of anything regarding Amy. I found something that you might be interested in. I'll be here until 6 this evening. Thanks.

He didn't want to get his hopes up unrealistically. He convinced himself that it was probably nothing; otherwise, she might have just called the police. On the other hand, if she had called the police, they might have simply dismissed her concern since they had gotten the word that a murder investigation would be bad for business. He put those thoughts aside as he entered Littleford Realty.

"Oh, hi there!" Kelli said with a warm smile. Bishop wondered if she had forgotten his name. "How are you enjoying your stay?"

"Love the cottage, but considering what happened to Amy, it's been a tough few days for me."

"I know exactly what you mean. I still can't believe it."

He had more questions for Kelli, but he really want to meet her boss.

"Is Ms. Littleford in?"

"Yes, she is." That probably explained why Kelli had avoided any negative comments about her. "Let me buzz her." She spoke softly into the phone. "Mr. Bishop is here to see you." After a brief pause, she smiled back at him. "Down that hallway. Second door on the right."

He knocked on the old wooden door. "It's open!" she barked.

Martha Littleford was sitting at a large desk covered with folders, binders, a stack of mail, and other papers. He stood in front of her desk, feeling like a student who was in for a stern lecture from the teacher. She finally shifted her focus away from her work, "Well, sit down." She looked to be in her eighties. Above each ear, she had clips in her long gray hair. Her skin was pale, wrinkled, and blotted with dark brown spots. Her hands were covered by a roadmap of veins, and her voice was low and gravelly. If a director were looking for someone to play the role of Miss Havisham from *Great Expectations* by Charles Dickens, Martha would have been a good choice. Spurned at the altar, the wealthy Havisham became a recluse who hated just about everything and everyone. All Littleford lacked was the bridal gown.

"My name is Michael Bishop and …"

She broke in mid-sentence. "I know who you are, and I know you want to talk to me about Amy Walsh." She looked directly at him with her small rheumy eyes. "Get to it. I'm busy."

"I appreciate your time," he said although he certainly didn't appreciate her attitude. He knew that *curmudgeon* usually referred to a man, but if ever he had met a female version, this woman was it. He knew that he had to get right to the point.

"Do you know why anyone would want to harm Amy?"

"No," she said bluntly. "The police have concluded that it was an accident. Why can't you accept that and move on?"

This was not a lady to be won over by charm. He decided to be blunt as well. "If Amy had simply slipped and fell, her body wouldn't have been wedged in the rocks the way it was. The police initially treated it as a suspicious death. In fact, since I was the one who found the body and my hat was found near the crime scene, I was briefly considered a suspect. However, for some reason, the police suddenly lost interest in the case."

Her crooked smile revealed her stained teeth as she spoke sarcastically, "Seems to me they did you a favor."

He chose to ignore her taunt.

She picked up some papers from her desk. "If there's nothing else ..."

"As a matter of fact, there is," he said defiantly. "I know that there was some tension between you and Amy because when she spoke to you on the phone Sunday night in my presence, she was asking you to let it go. What was that all about?"

She smiled that twisted smile again. "Too bad you didn't ask her when you had the chance."

He fought to control his anger at her callous remark. "It wouldn't have had anything to do with Amy challenging your sister for her seat on the Board of Selectmen, would it?"

Her face registered surprise that he knew about Amy's political ambitions. He was an outsider who had only been in town for a couple of days. "Oh, please!" she said as if the suggestion were ridiculous, "where do you come up with these crazy ideas? Miriam has never lost an election, and I can assure you that she isn't going to start now." She glared at him. "And just in case you're implying that my sister and I killed her to eliminate the competition, we were at a meeting in Biddeford that day, and we have witnesses that will testify to that."

"I'm sure you do," he said caustically, "but that doesn't mean that you didn't conspire with others to end her life ... and that of her unborn child." She seemed both upset and confused by his last remark. Was it his suggestion of a conspiracy that upset her? Was it his reference to Amy's pregnancy that confused her? Or both?

"Good day, Mr. Bishop," she said with an air of finality.

"Yes, I'm done here ..." he said as he opened her office door to leave. He looked back at her and added, "...for now," then shut the door firmly. As soon as he did, he remembered something else and decided not to waste the opportunity. He knocked on the door and without waiting for a reply, walked in. "I do have one more question," he announced. "If you knew you were going to be in Biddeford that day, why did you ask Kelli to come in early to meet a client who never showed up?"

The old woman started to laugh that turned into an extended coughing spell. When she caught her breath, she said, "Apparently, Kelli doesn't realize that she isn't supposed to discuss office business with anyone. I'll have to have a chat with her." She seemed to enjoy the prospect of disciplining her employee.

"Don't blame her," Bishop replied. "She didn't offer any details. I was the one who pressed her about it." He didn't remember if that was exactly the way it happened, but he wanted to protect Kelli from her boss's wrath. "And you didn't answer my question. Why did you instruct Kelli to be here in the office, when you knew that Amy would be alone on her run that morning?"

She pointed her gnarled finger at him. "I don't appreciate you coming in here and insinuating that I had anything to do with that woman's death. Now, get out before I call the police!"

He briefly explained to Kelli what just happened in Littleford's office, and he apologized for getting her into trouble. She waved it off as if it were not a problem. "I've worked here for eight years. I know what she's like. Don't worry about it!"

***

Once outside, he started walking along the busy sidewalk. In her text, Carole indicated that she found something that he ought to see. It felt good to be out of the oppressive atmosphere of that woman's office. He hoped that Littleford wouldn't fire Kelli, and Bishop appreciated her reassuring response to his warning. The old woman confirmed Kelli's explanation as to why she hadn't accompanied her friend on her jog that morning. He liked Kelli. In many ways, she reminded him of Terry, the school's secretary. He didn't consider her to be a suspect any longer.

Martha Littleford was another story. Based on her responses and her attitude, he was more inclined to believe that she was involved in Amy's death. However, she couldn't have acted alone. It was possible that her sister, Miriam, and Miriam's husband, Ray Gladstone, had formed a diabolical triumvirate. He also realized that by the time he had an opportunity to talk to the Gladstones, Martha would have filled them in on her morning encounter with him.

As he strolled back down Shore Road, the sidewalk became less crowded. He noticed a bicyclist up ahead weaving his way between cars and pedestrians, but didn't pay too much attention. He heard the cyclist stop near him.

"Hello, Mr. Bishop!"

His first thought was that it was someone from Holy Trinity. Who else would call him "Mister Bishop"? He just hoped that he would get the name right. He was surprised when he looked at the rider, one foot resting on the curb.

"Kiki! Nice to see you!" He reached out to shake the redhead's hand. Apparently, helmets weren't required in Maine.

"Same here."

"Where'd you get that bike?" The brakes were on the handles, and rusty fenders covered the wide tires. To complete the classic image, there was a wire mesh basket over the front tire, and streamers trailing in the breeze from the handlebars. It somehow looked familiar. Had he seen that bike before? As with so many other details of life lately, he couldn't quite remember. Perhaps it was just a flashback to the days of his youth.

"Picked it up at a yard sale. It's a beauty, isn't it?"

"Absolutely," said Bishop who was almost tempted to ask Kiki if he could take it for a spin. "What happened to your car?"

"Oh, that. That wasn't mine. I just borrowed it from a friend." Switching topics, he asked, "Where's Max?"

"He's back at the cottage."

"He's a real good dog."

Putting aside getting away from him and running onto the Marginal Way, Bishop had to admit that Max was a good dog who traveled well and liked classical music. "Yes, he is."

Kiki prepared to hit the road again. Before he left, he asked, "Is Minnehan still questioning you about that lady's death?"

"No, how about you?"

"Nah, I haven't heard nuthin' from him after that time in the hospital."

"I think that he's convinced that it was an accident."

"That's good because I knew you didn't do it. Well, I've gotta get going. Nice to see ya. Maybe next time, I'll get to see Max again."

He smiled and waved as Kiki pulled out into traffic, and continued on to the Belvedere Inn. He doubted that Carole had discovered anything of importance, but he needed to be sure. She was clearly uncomfortable when they last spoke. Was she hiding something?

He arrived to an empty lobby and Carole perched on a chair behind the counter as if she had been waiting for him. She waved him over. "Hello, Carole. I got here as quickly as I could. What's up?" He took his baseball cap off and placed it on the counter.

She reached down to get something. "We kept her office closed for a few days because we thought someone would come to claim her personal belongings. Since I've taken on her responsibilities, I need to use her office. With my morning schedule, I've even started jogging the beach or the path the way she did. Today I decided to pack everything up. That's when I found this."

Bishop picked up the crumpled piece of paper by the edges and read the one sentence written on it in thick black marker. There was something odd about the paper itself, but he focused on the disturbing message. *I'm not taking NO for an answer!* "Do you know who wrote this?"

"No idea," she quickly replied.

Bishop thought it strange that that was her response. The other day, she tried to suggest that David Conway, one of Amy's ex-boyfriends, was the type who might have been driven to lash out. Was it possible that Carole wrote the note in order to deflect attention from herself? Since the police had concluded that it was an accident, why would she bother?

"Where was it, exactly?"

"In the wastebasket."

"Why did you even bother to open a crumpled piece of paper that had been thrown away?" He knew that she probably didn't appreciate the grilling, but he wanted answers.

Carole was a bit defensive. "Well, we have a shredder for important stuff, and none of the other trash was scrunched up like that. I could see there was something written on it. I guess I just was curious."

"Have you shown this to anyone else?"

"No. Since you were asking so many questions about Amy's death, I thought that this might mean something."

Bishop didn't want to jump to conclusions. The note might have been totally unrelated to her death. On the other hand, he wondered if it might be enough to convince Minnehan and his superiors to open a more thorough investigation.

"Do you mind if I take this with me?"

She shrugged. "You can have it. It sort of gives me the creeps, anyway."

"Do you have an envelope that I could use?"

She went into the back and emerged a moment later with a large brown envelope. Bishop carefully slipped the paper into the envelope and fastened the metal clasp. It was unlikely, but perhaps a fingerprint analysis might reveal the identity of the person who wrote that note.

"Would you mind if I looked through her other personal effects?"

Carole placed the small bell on the counter. Luckily, the inn was unusually quiet as only a couple of guests had passed through, and there had been no calls. He followed her into a small office not far from the lobby itself. Once inside, he felt oddly uncomfortable as if he were trespassing. He insisted that Carole stay in the room as he looked through the carton that she had placed in a corner of the room next to some green filing cabinets.

He looked at each item trying to touch them as little as possible. There were some photos in frames of Amy with people that he did not recognize. In addition to some office supplies, there were various makeup items, breath mints, a twenty-dollar bill and some change, several pairs of earrings, and a pair of running shoes. The item of most interest was her desk calendar that he took out of the box to examine more closely. As he turned the pages, he was disappointed to see that there were very few notations, and the ones that were there didn't appear to be relevant.

"Did she have another calendar?"

The question disrupted the silence and caught Carole off guard. "I'm not really sure. She probably kept most of her appointments on her phone. That's what I do."

Bishop knew that she was probably right. However, the information on that phone was inaccessible. It occurred to him that there might be important clues at Amy's home. He made a mental note to look into the possibility of gaining access with or without the help of the police. Then he noticed something that stopped him in his tracks. She had made a notation for Monday, the day that she died.

Lunch with Mr. B. this week! It pained him to realize that he would never have that opportunity. He had only a couple of days left to find out who had taken her life. Was he deluding himself that such an accomplishment was possible?

He thanked Carole for her assistance, promised to check in with her again before he left Ogunquit, and headed for the door.

"Wait! Mr. Bishop!" Had she suddenly thought of something else that might be important? He spun around quickly.

"You forgot your hat."

"It's not the first time."

Chapter Fourteen

When he arrived at the cottage, Max greeted him energetically. Ron was eating a dish of ice cream and watching a rerun of *Judge Judy*. How nice it would be to determine who was telling the truth and who was lying within thirty minutes. Bishop, however, still had more questions than answers, and time was running out.

Ron muted the television as Bishop with a glass of lemonade in hand explained what happened since lunch. The crumpled note that Carole found was potentially the most significant finding of the day. There was something else about that note that bothered him, but he couldn't put his finger on it. He thought of the note from Ron that he had found on the kitchen counter that morning. He had crumpled that and tossed it. Perhaps this note simply had nothing to do with Amy's death. He hoped that he could convince Minnehan to come to a different conclusion.

He had other people that he wanted to talk to as well. He might find Miriam Littleford at the town hall, or at least, someone there would know where to find her. Her husband, Ray, was another person that he wanted to interview. And then there was Dave Conway, the man that Amy had recently fired, and the man with the reflector sunglasses whom Bishop had disturbed as he sat near the footbridge on the path where Amy died. He wanted to ask each of them a few questions. If he could get Minnehan's cooperation, he might be able to accomplish those objectives.

Max sat next to Ron instead of his owner in the hopes that he would get a taste of Ron's ice cream, or more likely, another taste.

Bishop took off his sneakers and socks and began to relax a little bit after what had been a hectic day. He and Ron decided to stay put for dinner. There were a couple of steaks in the fridge that Ron could slap on the grill.

The local news from Portland came on, and Ron put the volume back up. The lead story concerned the closing of one lane of a section of the Maine Turnpike for repaving. Nothing at all about Amy.

Muting the television again, Ron announced, "I had another call from Terry."

"What now?" asked, unsure what could be worse than the return of Sister Ann followed closely by the return of Sister Pat under questionable circumstances.

"Cheryl Hearst quit."

Nothing that happened at Holy Trinity really surprised him anymore, and with his investigation picking up steam as he ran out of time, it wasn't a top priority, but he asked, "Did she say why?"

"When Cheryl found out that Sister Ann had returned as the principal, she decided that she wanted out. Before Terry transferred the call, Cheryl told her that, rather than confronting the principal with her grievances, she was simply going to say that she had decided to pursue other opportunities."

Cheryl had been teaching social studies for a few years, and both men considered her a good person and a dedicated and effective teacher. When she first arrived, she had agreed to teach a creative writing class on a temporary basis. She had been teaching that class ever since. Even though she was a writer herself, she preferred classes in her own discipline. Ron had promised her that if he became the principal, he would address the situation. Once it became clear that that wasn't going to happen, she made her decision.

"It's really late to find a replacement, and I hate to see a good teacher leave," Bishop said. "Do you think it would make a difference if we both talked with Cheryl?"

"I thought of that, too, but she told Terry that she had already placed her letter of resignation in the mail."

"Terry could always intercept it," Bishop mused.

"That doesn't sound like you," Ron admonished.

"I guess you're right." Perhaps some of the devious dealings of Mayhem and Meany had begun to affect his judgment. He also learned over the last couple of years, that some degree of deceitfulness helped in several murder investigations. "I'll miss Cheryl."

Ron agreed. "But that's not the whole story."

Bishop wondered how much damage Sister Ann could do in just a few days. "What else?" he asked, not really sure that he wanted to know.

"Sister had Terry set up interviews for the social studies position with three people from the applications she had on file."

"Sounds reasonable given the time restraints," he replied cautiously expecting that there was more to it than that.

"Yeah, it does. The problem is with that creative writing class. Sister doesn't expect Cheryl's replacement, whoever that is, to have to deal with that."

"She didn't mind making Cheryl deal with it year after year," Bishop said, pointing out the obvious irony. Starting to panic, he asked, "She's not planning to drop that class, is she?"

"No, she told Terry that she was going to get Charlie Mitchell to do it."

Bishop put his head in his hands as if he had a sudden headache. "Good luck with that," he said as much to himself as to his friend.

"You know as well as I do that Charlie is always looking for ways to ingratiate himself with Sister Ann, and he probably won't mind the extra cash, either." He was rather proud of himself for coming up with that analysis.

"True on both counts, but you're forgetting one important fact."

"What's that?"

"Charlie will shortchange all of the kids signed up for that class. He's probably combing online sources right now looking for a year's worth of lesson plans."

Ron silently agreed and turned to one of his favorite topics. "I'm going to fire up that grill. Where are those steaks?"

***

They had dinner out on the second floor deck. For Bishop, it was a rare moment to simply relax and enjoy the beauty of his surroundings. That was his intention when he decided to drive up to Ogunquit in the first place. Much had changed in the few days since his arrival.

Bishop knew that his first order of business on Thursday was another visit to the police station. Using the note that Carole had found, he hoped to convince Minnehan to open a murder investigation. If that happened, he could return home on Saturday hoping that justice for Amy and her unborn child would be served. He also wanted to talk with Ray Gladstone of the Friends of the Marginal Way. The more he thought about it, the more likely it seemed that Gladstone, his wife Miriam, and his sister-in-law Martha were responsible. They had the most to gain. With Amy out of the way, Miriam would coast to another term on the Board of Selectmen. Clearly, Martha and Amy had a strained relationship. Was it possible that Amy had discovered some evidence of wrongdoing in her business transactions? Amy's death would prevent any damage to her financial empire. Also, Martha had arranged for Amy to be running alone that morning. And with Ray's influence, any suggestion that her death was suspicious would never gain any traction. And if they didn't commit the deed themselves, perhaps they had hired someone to do it. David Conway and the man with the reflective sunglasses were two possibilities.

Before they had even finished dinner, Ron said, "Let's go to Bessie's for lunch tomorrow."

Knowing Ron's preoccupation with food, his suggestion didn't come as much of a surprise. "Sure ... whatever," he replied unenthusiastically. He had hoped that Ron might be a bit more focused on issues that mattered most.

"I've been thinking about your hat."

Perplexed, Bishop asked, "My Red Sox cap?"

"No, no … your Tilley. You seem pretty sure that you lost it at Bessie's. I wonder if we can convince Orjana to give us a list of names of customers who paid with a credit card on Sunday night."

Bishop, feeling guilty for doubting Ron, responded to his suggestion. "Number one, I wouldn't want Orjana to get in trouble for trying to help us. Number two, even if we discovered that one of our suspects was there, that wouldn't prove that person stole my hat. And number three, what about customers who paid with cash?"

"Three strikes. I'm out!" Ron said with a laugh. "I guess I'm not cut out for this detective work."

"Nonsense. I've watched you solve dozens of problems at school."

"Yeah, but none of them involved a murder."

"Well, let's plan on lunch there tomorrow anyway."

***

After dinner, Ron turned on the television to watch the Sox game. He settled in on the sofa in the living room with a bowl of pretzels, a drink, and Max by his side hoping to scavenge some crumbs. Bishop went into the porch, sat in the comfortable chaise, turned on a lamp, and began reading a book by one of his favorite mystery writers, Donna Leon. He remembered that he had tossed several library books into the trunk assuming that he was going to have ample time for relaxation. In Leon's books, Luigi Brunetti, Commissario of Police in Venice, Italy, solves the most sinister crimes by methodically peeling away layers of lies, corruption, and greed while dealing with the incompetence of his superior, Vice Questore Patta, and others. However, on this night, Bishop found it difficult to concentrate on his reading as the real-life mystery of Amy's death kept surging to the forefront of his thoughts. Bishop could only wish that he had a fraction of the investigative skills of the fictional Brunetti.

Ron, trailed by Max, walked in and asked, "Why don't we go out for some ice cream?"

"What about the ball game?"

"They're already behind 6 – 1. I don't understand why the manager didn't take Buchholz out of the game sooner. He obviously didn't have his stuff tonight."

"Okay, then. Let's go." Then he turned to Max who appeared to be listening intently to the conversation. "You, too, buddy."

Just as they were about to leave, Bishop's cell buzzed. He took one look at the screen, exhaled deeply, and announced, "It's Charlie."

"Don't answer it," Ron advised. "He's probably going to brag about how he saved the day by agreeing to teach that creative writing class."

"You're probably right, but I might as well listen to it now and get it over with. You can drive."

Charlie was about fifty years old, a bachelor, and one of the veteran teachers on the staff of Holy Trinity. Unfortunately, he looked at teaching more as a job than as a profession. He often sought shortcuts to avoid the really hard work of teaching, and more often than not, he managed to avoid any repercussions. If the teacher was coasting, so were the students, and most of them didn't mind. The few who did were quietly switched into another teacher's class. It was Charlie who first used Mayhem and Meany to describe the administrative duo of Sister Ann and Sister Pat. Privately, he often complained, criticized, and ridiculed them in a merciless manner. Of course, in their presence, he took every opportunity to ingratiate himself with them, praising their every move, bringing them flowers and food (food mostly with Sister Pat in mind), and giving them gifts on their birthdays and at Christmas. Most of the faculty waited for the day when his Jekyll and Hyde routine would fail him.

"I hope I didn't catch you at a bad time," Charlie said.

"Well, actually, I'm in Maine for a few days." He wondered if Charlie already knew that. Regardless, it would give him a good reason to keep the conversation short.

"Getting away from it all before we start another school year?"

"Something like that," Bishop replied. He wasn't about to explain what transpired in the few days that he had been in Ogunquit. It was fine with him if Charlie and the others never found out. He could trust Ron to keep quiet. He made a mental note to ask

142

Terry to do the same, unless as was possible, she was already spreading the word.

Charlie's tone of voice shifted when the preliminaries concluded. "Guess who's going to be teaching Creative Writing this year?"

"Cheryl Hearst, I suppose." It was the obvious answer to a question about which he theoretically didn't know anything.

"Not anymore. She quit! I'm going to be doing it."

"Really? I wonder why Cheryl quit. I'll certainly miss her," he said which was a true statement. Then he added, "Congratulations!" which he tried to say with enthusiasm.

"Are you kidding? I'm totally peeved about it!"

Bishop had no choice except to ask, "Why?"

"I'll tell you why," he shot back as his anger bubbled over. "Now that Mayhem is back in charge, and incidentally I heard Meany is back as well, she is back to playing games."

Bishop listened, knowing that Charlie wouldn't need prompting to vent his frustrations. His only hope was that Ron would soon find an ice cream stand so that he would have a legitimate excuse to end the call.

"She told me that she checked schedules for the upcoming year, and I was the only teacher free to take on the new class." Choosing him to teach the class because there was no one else available to do it was far from a ringing endorsement. Apparently, she had deftly given him two unpleasant options – either accept a

143

class that he didn't want to teach or anger the principal right before the start of the year.

Looking on the bright side, Bishop offered this plus. "At least, you'll be making some extra cash. That always helps." Knowing that Charlie often claimed to be on the brink of financial ruin, he thought that he would gladly accept the extra class while putting in a minimal amount of effort. It was the students in that class who would suffer.

"Are you kidding, Michael? I guess I didn't make myself clear. She expects me to take on an extra class, but my salary will remain the same!"

"Now, you're the one who must be kidding." How could Sister Ann expect him to agree to that proposal? During the months of her suspension, Bishop tried to block some of her more outrageous behaviors from his memory. Sister Estelle had only reinstated her a few days earlier, and she was already falling back into her familiar patterns. When was Ron going to stop the car? Bishop felt a wave of sadness sweep over him as he contemplated the prospect of another year with Mayhem. And it would only be a matter of time, he assumed, before Meany would join in. He considered the possibility that Sister Pat might have actually been the one behind this maneuver.

Ron gave his friend a worried look just from listening to half of the conversation. Bishop made a rapid motion with his right hand indicating that Ron should hurry up and find a place to stop.

"I wish I were kidding, old pal, but I have been royally shafted."

"I'm so sorry, Charlie. I wish there were something I could do." He meant what he said. Although Charlie's own eagerness to please the administration might have set him up for this request, Bishop realized that the principal had now set a dangerous precedent that might have repercussions for other teachers down the road.

Finally, Ron pulled into Benson's Ice Cream stand somewhere along Route 1. Even Max seemed relieved that they had arrived at their destination. The parking lot was packed, and there were long lines at both windows for ordering. Ron always thought that a crowd meant good food.

"Listen, Charlie, I really must be going. Maybe you'll end up enjoying that class."

"Maybe … but I'm not in the habit of working for free." He sounded resigned to his fate.

"I'll be back in a few days. Talk to you soon."

Ron was interested in what Charlie had to say, but he was more interested in getting in line. "You stay here with Max. Just tell me what you want."

He thought for a moment. "I'll have small black cherry cone and get a small vanilla soft serve in a cup for Max but ask them to make it very small." When he spotted an unoccupied wooden bench, he jumped out of the car with Max on a short leash, and headed that way. He signaled to Ron who was still waiting in line where to find them.

Ron joined them at the bench holding a cardboard box with their desserts. Max soon was licking his mouth as his small serving disappeared quickly. Bishop, always the slow eater, was trying to keep up with the dripping ice cream on the sides of the cone. Ron didn't have much to say as he tackled a huge banana split. When Bishop finished, they cleaned up and got back in the car for the ride back to the cottage. Some pesky mosquitoes prevented Bishop from sitting out on the upstairs deck to watch the water change colors as the light faded. He could not help but wonder if his chances of finding Amy's killer were also fading.

Chapter Fifteen

When Bishop walked into the police station, the young African American woman with the beautifully braided hair smiled, picked up the phone to call Minnehan, and waved him through the security system. "He's on his way down," she said pleasantly. Bishop was relieved that he wouldn't have to sit in the uncomfortable plastic chair in the stifling room with one dreary window. He was hopeful this meant that Minnehan was ready to talk. Either that or he was going to give him one last warning about meddling.

As they walked out into the refreshing early morning air, Bishop contemplated how he should begin. He had the crumpled sheet of paper with the threatening message on it that Carole found in Amy's wastebasket. Should he start with that? Should he try to find out more about Ray Gladstone and why he seemed to have so much influence in town affairs?

When he looked at Minnehan, those questions were superseded by a sudden realization. In addition to wearing his everyday uniform, Minnehan had put on a pair of wraparound reflective sunglasses. Bishop felt a sudden chill despite the morning sun. Was it possible? As a teacher, he knew that students were often thrown off guard when they saw Bishop wearing something other than his typical school clothing. He had only seen Minnehan in his uniform. Did Minnehan don the sunglasses as a test? Bishop decided that he didn't have much to lose. "You're the man at the footbridge that I stumbled upon at the footbridge the other day!"

"I knew that you'd figure it out sooner or later," he replied. He seemed relieved that he would be able to tell his story.

"You must have recognized me. Why did you take off like that?"

"Because I *did* recognize you, and I was embarrassed more than anything else. I knew that you'd want to know what I was doing there."

"Given the circumstances, I think that I might have done the same thing." Bishop spoke in a conversational rather than confrontational tone. Over the years, he had found that he often achieved better results with that approach.

As they walked along Main Street, some of the locals greeted the officer as they passed. Invariably, they glanced at the stranger with whom Minnehan was walking, wondering if he was being interrogated. In fact, the opposite was true.

"I really don't know why I went there that morning. There was nothing I could do. I lost someone that I cared about and the baby that she was carrying, and there was nothing I could do about it."

"Because of Gladstone's interference?"

Ron simply nodded.

"Do the Friends of the Marginal Way have that much power"?

"It's Ron himself and a small circle of very wealthy and well-connected people. They run this town, and don't appreciate anyone getting in their way."

"You make them sound pretty ruthless."

"They are," he replied without elaboration.

"Do you think that Amy's decision to run against Gladstone's wife might have made them feel threatened in some way, and that they might have decided to stop her?"

Minnehan stopped and turned to Bishop. "I didn't know that Amy was running for anything." He seemed truly caught off guard.

"She didn't tell you?"

"No. How did you know?"

"Kelli Dempsey, the secretary at Littleford Realty told me. Apparently, they jogged together most mornings except the morning of the death when her boss ordered Kelli to get to the office early."

"Her boss? You mean Martha Littleford ... The Ogre of Ogunquit?"

"I haven't heard that one."

"She's been called a lot worse than that," he said without adding any details. He clearly was considering the possibilities. "I guess the three of them might have cooked up some scheme, but I don't see how they actually could have pulled it off. They're all pretty old ... no offense."

"I hear what you're saying. I agree that they must have had help."

Bishop had thought that the man with the reflective sunglasses might have been that person. Perhaps he had revisited that spot having regretted his action. Knowing that that man was Minnehan, might he be considered a suspect? Could that be the

149

reason for his reluctance to pursue an investigation? Could he be using Ray Gladstone as an excuse? Could David Conway, the man that Amy had recently fired, have been angered enough to do the bidding of the Littleford – Gladstone trio? That was another possibility that Bishop had yet to examine.

Minnehan indicated that it was time for him to head back to the station. This seemed to be the right time to show the officer the note. He pulled it out of the envelope and handed it to him. He read it quickly. "Where did you get this?" For the first time since their walk started, he was clearly angry. "Withholding evidence is a crime, you know."

"How I acquired it isn't important. And if it is evidence, why isn't someone investigating the crime?"

Minnehan gave the note back to Bishop. "No sense testing for prints, I suppose," he said as he regained his composure. Bishop knew that the note might be completely irrelevant to Amy's fate. He realized that if Carole was involved, she might have used the note as a ruse to deflect attention from herself.

Bishop wasn't sure whether or not the note might be important to the investigation, but Minnehan was making it clear that, however much he might want to pursue it, he wasn't going to be allowed to proceed.

There was another angle that he wanted to pursue. He needed to ask a difficult question. "Any chance you weren't the father?"

Minnehan thought about it before he responded. "I suppose … but Amy said it was me, and I believe her."

"Let's just suppose that someone else thought he was the father. That might have provoked him to attack Amy. Do you have any idea who that might have been?"

"First of all, you're making some big assumptions that it was somebody else, that she told that person, and that he would have reacted violently."

"I agree, but I want to look at every possibility."

Minnehan took his sunglasses off and said quietly, "I appreciate what you're doing. I wish I could do more."

"I understand. Are you working tomorrow?"

"No, Friday is my day off. Why?"

"I've got an idea," Bishop said without elaborating, "and I might need your help."

"I'll do what I can … as long as it's legal."

Since Bishop wasn't a lawyer, he didn't comment on that one way or the other. Before Minnehan entered the building, he had one more question. "What did you pick up that morning that you put in your pocket?"

He smiled, reached into his uniform pants pocket, and pulled something out. He held it in his open palm for Bishop to see.

As he looked at a rather small stone with numerous specks of quartz sparkling in the light of the sun, he was totally confused. "Why this?"

"I don't know, really. I just saw it there where Amy lost her life, and I guess I just wanted to have something to remind me of her."

Then Bishop remembered that, years ago, he had kept a flower that had been on his wife's casket. It was a way to deal with the pain. "I understand," was all he said.

Just as the station door was about to close, Bishop remembered something.

"Wait a second!" he shouted.

Minnehan kept the door open as he waited for Bishop to tell him what he wanted.

"I almost forgot. I was hoping you might be able to tell me where I could find Ray Gladstone?"

The officer consulted his watch. "This time of day you might find him at Bessie's."

It was apparent to Bishop that just about all the locals could be found there at one time or another. He thought of the Latin words *mille viae ducunt homines per saecula Romam* that roughly translated to the expression, *All roads lead to Rome*. At school, Bishop delighted in the befuddled looks he would get from Sister Pat when he dropped some Latin phrase on her. He had assumed that her banishment to a soup kitchen far from Groveland meant the end of that entertainment. With the latest news from Terry, he was no longer so confident in that assessment. For the moment, his most important assessment lay before him. All roads lead to Bessie's.

***

Bishop entered the crowded restaurant and stood at the coat rack from which he was sure that someone had lifted his hat. As he scanned some of the customers, he wondered if one of them was the culprit. By planting that Tilley at the scene of the crime, had that person targeted him to take the fall for the crime, or was it simply a diversionary tactic perpetrated on an unsuspecting, absent-minded visitor?

After waiting a few moments for a seat to open up, Orjana greeted him with a smile. "Gud morninck, Meester Beeshop. Wan for breakfast?"

He was pleasantly surprised that she was working this shift. "I was wondering," he whispered, "if a man by the name of Ray Gladstone is here by any chance."

"Oh, yah. He's here just about every days. He just sat down by hisself in a booth in my section. Do you know heem?"

"No, but I know he is involved with the Friends of the Marginal Way. Would you please ask him if it would be okay if I joined him?"

She returned in a matter of seconds and motioned him to follow her. As he approached the booth, he saw an elderly man with a cup of coffee and a menu in front of him. He was mostly bald with tufts of shaggy gray hair on the sides. His wide nose was the dominant feature of his face. A pair of small rimless glasses perched on his nose. His expression was devoid of any friendliness.

"Meester Beeshop, this is Meester Gladstone," Orjana said as she placed a menu on the table for Bishop. "Tea?"

"Yes, please."

The two men shook hands. "I hear you want to make a major contribution to the Friends," said Gladstone as he stirred his coffee.

153

Bishop had no idea what Orjana had told him in order to get him to agree to share the table, so he played along. "Well, I have a great fondness for the Marginal Way. My wife and I used to come here every summer back in the day."

"Speaking of wives, I'm expecting mine here any minute," he said, obviously annoyed that she was late.

Bishop began to get up. "I'm so sorry. Orjana said … ah, well … I certainly didn't mean to interrupt your breakfast."

He motioned for Bishop to stay. "What breakfast? The wife's usually late." Then he added as if he were talking to an old buddy, "Always time for a little business, eh?" He made an odd sound that Bishop assumed was his attempt at laughter.

"I'll only take a few minutes of your time." He pushed the menu to the corner of the table. "I understand that you're the president of the Friends."

"That's right. Been with them for over thirty years," he said proudly.

"It certainly is one of the most famous landmarks in the area."

He made that same throaty sound. "You mean 'the world.' We literally have visitors from all over the globe."

"I didn't realize …" Bishop said although he certainly did.

"Yes, we've made many improvements over the years, and that costs money. We rely heavily on donations. Would you like to purchase a bench plaque? They're twenty-five grand."

154

The suggestion staggered him. What were the Friends doing with all of that money? "Well … I wasn't thinking of anything in that range," he responded as he felt his face flush. Just at that moment, he caught a glimpse of a cyclist passing by their window on the Main Street side of the building. It was a chance to change the subject, and he took it.

The red-haired rider and the bike with the wire basket and streamers were unmistakable. "That's Kiki!"

Gladstone leaned over to catch a glimpse. He shook his head disapprovingly. "You mean, Cuckoo."

Bishop intended to ask Gladstone a few questions about Amy's death before Mrs. Gladstone arrived, but his remark sparked his curiosity. "Why do say that?"

Again, that odd-sounding laugh. "That's what everybody calls him around here. He's a sad case. Must be close to thirty and still lives with Mama. Used to drive a school bus 'til he lost his license." He made a motion of lifting an imaginary glass to his mouth. "Now he rides around on that fool bike looking for a date." He looked around, and Bishop assumed that his wife had entered the restaurant. He pointed to the waitress. "Betcha he's asked Orjana out more than once."

Bishop was stuck on the fact that Kiki had lost his license, and yet he drove to the hospital after Bishop was stung and later offered him a ride back to his car. He did say that he "borrowed" the car he was driving. Turning his focus back to the task at hand, he knew that he had to seize the moment.

"Terrible tragedy out on the Marginal Way earlier this week," he said in a conversational tone.

"Accidents happen," he said dismissively. "Stay off the rocks. People need to pay attention to the signs." He looked at his watch again, obviously hoping that his wife would come in and rescue him from further discussion of this topic.

"From everything I've heard, she was jogging on the path. Accident? Are you sure it was an accident?"

"It happens once in a blue moon, but we have weddings there all the time."

"Has there ever been a murder on the Marginal Way?"

"Never," he replied bluntly.

"A murder would certainly put a crimp in the tourism industry, wouldn't it?"

He placed both hands around his cup, leaned forward toward Bishop, and said coldly, "You're not here to make a donation are you, Bishop?"

"I haven't decided yet," he replied defensively.

"Listen, I know who you are. You've been nosing around, asking too many questions for your own good."

"Is that a threat?"

Bishop never got to hear Gladstone's response as Mrs. Miriam L. Gladstone, long-time member of the town board, walked up to the booth. Her medium-length hair, about three shades too dark for a woman her age, was perfectly coiffed as if she just left the hairdresser. That might explain her tardiness. She was wearing a short-sleeved pink blouse, tan slacks, and a pair of dressy sandals. She was definitely classier than her husband.

"Hello, dear. This gentleman was just about to leave."

Bishop quickly rose and reached out to shake her hand. "Michael Bishop. Nice to meet you, Mrs. Gladstone." He gestured for her to sit down. She smiled politely.

Ray Gladstone didn't bother to shake Bishop's hand or even to look at him. As he began to walk away, he heard her ask, "What did he want?"

He looked back in their direction. "The truth," he said firmly. Bishop left the restaurant more convinced than ever that in his efforts to solve the mystery of Amy's death, he had stumbled into a wasps' nest, and if he wasn't careful, he was going to get stung.

Chapter Sixteen

Instead of heading back to the cottage, he decided to take a long walk on the beach. He crossed Main and went down Beach Street. At one end of a large parking lot, there was a row of benches facing the water with a long fabric awning overhead flapping in the wind. He sat down, removed his sneakers and socks, stuffed the socks in the sneakers, and decided to give Ron a quick call to let him know of his plans. He wondered why Ron didn't pick up, but left a brief message and started on his walk.

He had looked forward to taking such walks on this vacation, but circumstances transformed him from carefree tourist to amateur sleuth. He needed this time to think. It was clear to him that Amy Walsh and her unborn child had been killed. There was no way that her body would have ended up where he found it merely by tripping on the path. Since there was no evidence of a struggle, she must have known her attacker. Whoever it was had also left Bishop's Tilley hat there to shift focus elsewhere. That part of the plan failed as the police yielded to pressure from Ray Gladstone and dropped their fledgling investigation.

As for motive, a number of people might have wanted her out of the way. Martha Littleford and Amy had recently had some kind of a disagreement. He knew that much from the phone conversation that he overheard on his arrival in Ogunquit. Martha hadn't been willing to share much light on that topic. She did, however, admit to requiring Kelli to forego her morning jog that left Amy vulnerable to attack. Kelli knew of Amy's pregnancy and expressed some disdain for her friend's moral character. Not much motive for a criminal act, Bishop concluded, and unless she had left the office unattended, she wouldn't have had the opportunity either.

As he splashed along in ankle-deep water, he considered Amy's relationships with several men and their possible motivations. David Conway, whom she had recently fired and whom she had dated, was an unknown. Bishop had not yet talked with him. He might have been motivated by revenge for the loss of his job or by her rejection of him or both. Officer Ben Minnehan admitted that he was the father. At least, he thought he was. Might he have killed Amy in a rage over her infidelity? Was he really in love with her as he claimed, or did he kill Amy to avoid the responsibilities of fatherhood? Minnehan also admitted to being the man that Bishop had encountered sitting at the edge of the small footbridge where Amy died. Was he mourning her loss or assuaging a guilty conscience?

Another man that came to mind was Kiki Cavendish, or Cuckoo, if one listened to Ray Gladstone. What possible motive might he have? As far as Bishop knew, those two didn't even know each other. As for opportunity, he was helping Bishop chase Max who had run onto the Marginal Way. He was with him when Max led them to the crime scene. Amy had been dead for hours at that point, and Bishop knew that Kiki was the clerk at Hannaford's who brought out to his car a bag of groceries that he had left behind. That was approximately at the same time that Amy was pushed to her death.

Bishop decided that he had walked far enough and started to head back. The refreshing northerly breeze was no longer in his face. The sun felt noticeably hotter as he worked his way through other suspects. Carole Perrault became the manager of the Belvedere Inn after Amy's death. Might she have coveted that job enough to take drastic measures to get it? She seemed quite eager to suggest that David Conway was hot tempered and capable of violence. She also found a crumpled note in Amy's office wastebasket that suggested someone was upset with her. Again, he wondered if she had written the note herself.

Finally, from his recently concluded meeting with Ray Gladstone, the President of the Friends of the Marginal Way, other possibilities emerged. Why had Gladstone pressured the police to drop their investigation? Was it to protect the tourism industry, or did he have a more personal motive? Amy had filed papers to challenge his wife, Miriam L. Gladstone, for her seat on the town board. Politics was often a dirty game, and Ray seemed a rather nasty man. To keep his wife in office, to what depths might he have sunk? In addition, Miriam and Martha Littleford were sisters. All three seemed to benefit from Amy's "accident." It was possible that all of them hatched a plot, and if they couldn't execute it by themselves, they had the resources to get the job done. On the other hand, it was possible that one of the three acted alone. If so, which one? Martha and Miriam seemed unlikely to have confronted a much younger and more physically fit woman. That left Ray Gladstone who, in his connection with the Friends, would not have raised any suspicion if he was seen on the Marginal Way that foggy morning. He also knew every inch of the path better than anyone.

As he reached the benches, brushed the sand from his feet, and put on his socks and sneakers, he kept thinking of the look in Ray's eyes when he threatened Bishop. It reminded him of photos he had seen of Mafioso Jimmy Blades when he was on trial for murder.

***

When he spoke with Minnehan, he mentioned that he had an idea of how he might proceed. As he walked, he refined that idea into a tentative plan. There were still too many variables for his liking.

Back again on Main Street, he noticed a bookstore just a short distance away. The rectangular wooden sign had large gilded letters, *Book Emporium*. He had brought several books with him that were largely still unread at this point. He didn't plan on spending much time there, but he couldn't resist the allure of some quiet time browsing the shelves. As he opened the leaded glass door, a bell attached to the top rang loudly enough to alert the clerk that someone had entered. A young woman with blond hair held back by a plastic headband peaked out to greet him. Wearing a long sleeved oxford shirt with the tails untucked, jeans that were fashionably threadbare, and flats, she asked, "May I help you, sir?"

"No, thank you," he replied to this attractive attendant who needed no makeup to augment her natural beauty. "I just thought I would browse around for a few minutes."

"Well, if you have any questions, just ask. We have some discounted books on the display to your right." She went back to whatever work she was doing in the stacks.

As he took in the general layout of the place, he noticed a section dedicated to local authors. Some were unknown to him; others were very familiar, including Sarah Orne Jewett, a 19th century writer who lived in nearby South Berwick, and Celia Thaxter, one of whose books he had found at the cottage. As he continued to browse, he noticed a large stone fireplace flanked by several reading chairs. It would be a perfect spot to spend some time on a chilly autumn day.

He grabbed one of the newspapers from a side table and sank into one of the thickly cushioned chairs. He had been aware of some classical music playing in the background, and as he listened more carefully, he recognized a recording of Johann Sebastian Bach's *Keyboard Concerto No. 1 in D minor*. Settling back to enjoy some classical music that had been lacking during this week, he casually scanned yesterday's copy of *The Weekly Sentinel*. It was the same issue in which Ron found the brief notice indicating that Amy's name would remain on the ballot despite her death. Miriam L. Gladstone, the incumbent, would essentially be running unopposed.

Just as he was about to fold up the paper, another small article caught his attention. The Ogunquit Board of Selectmen had approved the application of Wellington Enterprises to build a six-unit upscale condominium on a lot on Atlantic Avenue that was formerly occupied by a duplex that had been destroyed by fire.

Despite opposition from some neighbors who expressed concerns about additional traffic, noise, and the fact that the proposed structure would change the character of the neighborhood, the resolution passed 3 – 2 with Miriam L. Gladstone casting the deciding vote.

As he opened the door to leave, the bell rang. The clerk appeared from nowhere to say, "Please, come in again." Bishop doubted that he would have time for that. The news item tucked away on a back page was very troubling. Mrs. Gladstone seemed to wield a lot of influence in town. He wondered how many times she had cast such deciding votes. He wondered about Wellington Enterprises. Was it possible that the wealthy realtor, Martha Littleford, had some connection to that company? This was perhaps just a hint of what harm a few powerful individuals could inflict on an otherwise idyllic small town. To untangle the extent of their business affairs might take a team of lawyers, accountants, and prosecutors many months. Bishop had only one more day to nail them on two counts of murder.

The idea that he had mentioned to Minnehan began to take the shape of a plan. It was a long shot, but it was all he had.

***

As he approached 89 Israel Head Road, he felt the vibration of the cell phone in his pocket. He assumed that it was Ron wondering what was going on. It was also close to lunchtime, and he had likely been researching their options.

He was wrong. Ron hadn't called. He had received a cryptic text from Terry. *Be prepared. Sister Ann is churning up the waters. Will call when the coast is clear.* He wondered if Terry had chosen her words mindful of the fact that he was at the beach. The principal had only resumed her duties a few days earlier. She seemed to be taking advantage of Ron's well-deserved mini-vacation to exert her authority. What was she up to this time? Whatever it was, he had a strong suspicion that the scooter-bound Sister Pat had played a significant role despite the fact that she had not been reinstated as assistant principal.

Ron was in the porch on the phone, presumably with Mary Ellen. Max charged into the kitchen hoping that his owner had brought home a treat. He settled for a few pieces of kibble. After cleaning up, Bishop sat down in the living room with a cold glass of lemonade.

Ron came in, popped a piece of saltwater taffy in his mouth, and managed to say, "Mary Ellen sends her love," as he worked the taffy like a wad of chewing tobacco. "Want one? There's a box on the kitchen counter."

"Maybe later,' he replied. Suddenly, he had a flashback to a rainy day years ago when he and Grace had made the short drive to York Beach. Wearing their slickers, they walked the deserted Short Sands, and then strolled the main street where they came upon a few people looking through the large window of a restaurant. This place made its own taffy, and people could watch the entire process unfold. Grace was fascinated to watch the flavors poured into the

164

vats and the large rotating metal arms work the mixture to the correct consistency. It was a brilliant advertising strategy as those who stopped to watch the process invariably went in to buy some taffy to take home. Nothing that Ron purchased could compare to the taffy that he remembered from those days.

After filling Ron in on his morning meeting with Officer Minnehan, he described his testy exchange with Ray Gladstone, and his accidental discovery of Mrs. Gladstone's recent controversial vote on a construction project. He shared everything with his friend except the details of the plan that he was still formulating.

"Sounds as if you've had quite a morning. It's not every day you get threatened by one of the town's heavyweights," he said, trying to balance his attempt at humor with his genuine concern for his friend's well-being.

Turning his thoughts back to the officer, he asked Bishop, "I wonder why Minnehan was so quick to give up the investigation that personally meant so much to him. Do you think he'd roll over just because Gladstone told him it would be bad for business? Do you think he's on the take?"

He paused for a moment before answering. "No, I don't, but I wouldn't be surprised if someone higher up is. The chief, for example, must be approved by the selectmen, and Gladstone's wife obviously would have some say in that decision."

"That might be one of the reasons that Amy had decided to run against Mrs. Gladstone. Perhaps she had stumbled onto some evidence of corruption."

Bishop sipped the last of the lemonade. "You might be right. Unfortunately, I don't know exactly whose feathers she had ruffled."

Ron unwrapped another piece of taffy, but before he popped it into his mouth, he said mysteriously, "I made a bit of a discovery myself, this morning."

"Really?" Bishop replied, not knowing whether Ron had discovered another restaurant that they simply had to try, or if he had picked up some information that might be helpful to his investigation.

After working the taffy for a moment, he managed to explain. "Yeah, I was looking at some box scores from last night's games, and I saw that the Mets had brought up a rookie by the name of Conway."

"That couldn't be David Conway," he said dismissively. Bishop was disappointed. He was hoping that Ron had stumbled onto something important. He should realize that the David Conway who was just fired by Amy only days ago could not possibly be the Mets rookie player.

"Of course not," Ron replied, his ego somewhat bruised. "But it got me thinking about how we could find this guy, and I looked up all the Conways listed on whitepages.com."

Bishop listened with renewed faith in his friend. "Go on."

"Well, there were seven, and I hit the jackpot on the fourth call. I spoke with this lady, Geraldine Conway who lives in Eliot, not too far from here. I told her that Dave and I were college buddies, and since I was in town for a few days, I thought we might get together. I added that I knew he worked at the Belvedere, but when I went there, they said he left, and they didn't know where he was."

Bishop shook his head in disbelief. "What if David hadn't gone to college? That would have been the end of that."

"Didn't think of that," he admitted, "but it worked out okay."

"Did you find out how to locate this guy?"

"Yup. He's at the Maplewood Restorative Center in Lenox, Mass."

"Rehab?"

"Yup. Granny said that his drinking was the reason he lost his job at the inn, and he realized that it was time to get back on the right track."

"When did he go?"

"Last Saturday. If that's true, he's not our man."

"That's a big 'if.' Maybe David coached Granny on what to say if anyone started asking questions." Bishop got up to go to the kitchen. He decided to ask for Officer Minnehan's help in verifying what Ron was told. That would accomplish two things. Not only would he be able to eliminate Dave as a suspect, it would also prove to him that Minnehan was willing to follow through on his promise to help in any way that he could.

"There's one more thing I learned today," Ron said.

His interest piqued, he sat back down. Bishop had forgotten the vaguely disturbing text that he had received from Terry. He hoped that it didn't have anything to do with Holy Trinity. "What's that?"

167

"Well, I was walking Max around the neighborhood, and there was a landscaping crew working on this place on Stearns Road. It must be one of the pricier estates up here. The house, a two-story stucco with blue shutters, sits well back from the road, but I got a good enough look at it … must have five or six bedrooms … and a tremendous view."

Bishop wondered whether he had missed something or not. Ron said that he had learned something. Had he suddenly become interested in the real estate market? He realized that his friend sometimes took the long way around a story, so he decided to let him continue without rushing him.

Ron opened a bag of pretzels that he must have picked up this morning. He tilted the open bag toward Bishop who waved it away. "Anyway, I started talking with one of the guys who was laying new sod near some hedges along the street. He took a liking to Max … very friendly guy about fifty years old… in great shape … Frankie Tataglia. I made a comment about the impressive house, and he said, 'You should see the pool house. I swear I could live in there.'" The pretzels must have made him thirsty as he grabbed a soda from the fridge, popped it open, and took a drink before he continued.

Bishop assumed that Ron was getting closer to the point. "I noticed that the truck the guys were using was a Town of Ogunquit vehicle so I asked him if they took on jobs for town residents. 'Hell, no! We're too busy for that, but this here place belongs to the

Gladstones, and when they need something done, we hop right over.'"

"The Gladstones? As in Raymond and Miriam L. Gladstone?"

"They're the ones. Frankie said that the property was once used a rental for the rich and famous. Nixon stayed there for a month when he was vice president."

"We know that Miriam comes from money, but what about Ray? I wonder what he does for a living."

Smiling with pride, he said, "As a matter of fact, I casually asked Frankie that very question, and he told me that Ray owned a construction company that did a lot of business with the town and with York County as well." He winked as he added, "I do some stuff for him when he asks."

"Good work. Seems the Gladstones might be taking advantage of their position to wrangle some free labor from the maintenance department. Given her position in town government and his business interests, it wouldn't surprise me that they have bent or broken a few laws along the way."

Ron completed his report on his morning findings. "As Frankie gave Max one last scratch behind his ears, he told me that after they finished up there, they were headed to the next place up the street. He said that was an even nicer than this one. Guess who owns that one?"

Bishop didn't hesitate. "Martha Littleford."

"You got it!" Ron reached out to give Bishop a high five.

Chapter Seventeen

"I think that we've made some real progress this morning. How about some lunch?"

Ron immediately jumped up to grab his keys. "My thoughts exactly, and I found another great place to try."

"Hold on a sec," Bishop quickly replied as he remembered a few items that needed attention. "Would you mind taking Max for a short walk before we leave? I need to make a couple of calls."

Ron readily agreed. He never had a pet of his own as a kid, and Max was an easy dog to like. He knew that he would miss having that Jack Russell around when he got back to Groveland. On the other hand, he missed Mary Ellen, and he was fairly sure that she wasn't interested in having a pet of any kind.

Sitting in the chaise on the front porch, Bishop called Minnehan. He explained that he needed some help in tracking down David Conway, a man who might have had a couple of reasons to harm Amy Walsh. As the manager of the Belvedere Inn, she had recently fired him. She also had dated him at one time, and there might have been lingering resentment over that. Bishop gave the officer the name of the rehab facility in Lenox where Conway was supposedly undergoing treatment. If that were verified, Conway would be eliminated as a suspect.

"Where did you get this information?"

Bishop hesitated. He didn't want to implicate Ron in any possible wrongdoing. "I'd rather not say," he answered, hoping that Minnehan wouldn't pursue the point.

"What do you want me to do?" That was the response that Bishop had been hoping for.

"Talk to this guy and the folks that run that place and verify that he was, in fact, there on Monday."

"I'll see what I can do."

"One more favor?"

"What's that?"

"I need that information ASAP. I'm leaving on Saturday, and I need to make something happen tomorrow."

"What do you mean by that?"

"I'm not quite sure yet, but I'll let you know as soon as I can. I'm going to need your help then as well."

Minnehan seemed skeptical but agreed to get back to him on Conway.

Bishop felt that there was something else he wanted to ask of Minnehan, but he couldn't recall what it was. He thought that if he didn't obsess over it, it might come back to him. He focused on the next call that he knew would be even more difficult. He called Littleford Realty, and Kelli answered cheerfully. When he identified himself, she said that she was sorry, but that the boss was out of the office.

"That's perfect! You're the one that I wanted to talk to."

"Me?" She asked nervously. Perhaps she feared that this kindly older gentleman was about to ask her out.

"Kelli, are you still jogging in the morning?"

***

Bishop finished his calls and sat back for a moment to reflect on his situation. His return to the sea, the place where life on this planet began, and to Ogunquit in particular, the place where he and Grace shared so many wonderful moments, had a tremendous pull on him. In only a couple of days, he would be returning to his home on the hill in Groveland. He knew as well that he would feel a sense of comfort there as if renewing acquaintance with an old friend. The question that burned in him was whether or not he would be able to bring to justice the individual or individuals who took the life of his former student, Amy Walsh, and that of her unborn child. He had begun to put in motion a last ditch effort to bring about that result. He had no idea if it would work, but he had to try something. It was the least he could do.

When Ron returned with Max, he saw that his friend had finished making his calls. He didn't ask who he had called or why. He trusted that he would tell him what he needed to know when he needed to know it.

The short walk with the dog had only increased his appetite. "Shall I drive?" Ron asked.

"Not this time, I'm afraid." He knew that Ron must have already selected not only the restaurant but probably also what he had planned to order. "Let's walk to Bessie's."

"Bessie's? Again? I mean I like that place, but don't you want to try someplace different?" He was trying not to sound too argumentative, but food selection was important to him.

"Normally, I'd be all for it, but I really need to talk with Orjana again. I just hope that she's there."

As the two men walked down Shore Road, they were unusually quiet. It had been a productive morning for both of them, and neither knew what the rest of the day would bring. Just as they arrived at the restaurant, Bishop's cell rang. His initial reaction was to ignore it, but then he realized that it might be Minnehan or Kelli or Carole or perhaps even Raymond Gladstone wanting to reaffirm his threat. When he shielded the screen from the bright sun, he realized that it was Terry from school. In her message earlier that morning, she mentioned something about Sister Ann and that she would call when she had an opportunity.

"It's Terry," he told Ron. "Why don't you go in and get a booth for us? Make sure that Orjana is our waitress. I'll be in in a few minutes."

Luckily, one of the benches in the shade in front of Bessie's was unoccupied. He sat down and took the call. She asked him how his investigation was going. He told her that the jury was still out on that, but that he would know more within the next twenty-four hours.

"I take it that Sister Ann is out of the building at the moment."

"Yup. She and Sister Pat are having lunch at *The Commodore*," one of the most expensive restaurants in town.

"Really? I hope they're not dipping into petty cash again," he joked, although he knew it was no laughing matter.

"No need to … this time," she said teasingly.

"What do you mean?"

"Our buddy, Charlie Mitchell, who's always complaining that he doesn't have a dime to his name, showed up a little while ago, and whisked them off. He invited me as well, knowing that I couldn't leave the office."

Charlie was known for playing up to the administrators at every opportunity while trashing Mayhem and Meany behind their backs. Bishop thought for a moment. What was his colleague in the English department up to? It didn't take him long to come up with a theory.

"I'll wager my next paycheck that he's going to wrangle his way out of taking on that extra class."

"Sheesh! If he pulls that off, somebody else is in for a big surprise."

Bishop wanted to keep the call short. Before she had a chance to go on about Charlie, Bishop asked, "Is that what your text was about?"

"Nah. Lunch with Charlie is nothing compared to what else is going down. It's been a busy week for her," she said sarcastically.

"Well, what's up?"

"Plenty."

"Like what?"

Terry blurted out, "Sister Ann is sending a letter out to all of the faculty tomorrow explaining that because of Sister Pat's physical limitations she expects everyone to pick up the slack."

Bishop responded, "What slack? Sister Pat didn't really have any duties, did she?"

When Terry stopped laughing, she said, "Well, according to this letter, teachers will be assigned to cover afternoon detentions, hall monitoring, and cafeteria duties."

"Teachers already do all of that."

"Now they'll have even more assignments … and that's not all. Homeroom teachers are going to be responsible for lockers for their students. They will also be expected to monitor their charges at all dances and games, etc."

"You're kidding me! Can you imagine how that will go over? We might lose another teacher or two right before the start of the school year. We already lost Hearst because of the principal's reinstatement. You would think that she might not want to rock the boat too soon."

"Rock the boat? She's capsized it if you ask me. She's sending the letter out on Friday, hoping that people will calm down by Monday."

"She's used that technique before." Bishop's curiosity got the best of him. "I'm sure that Sister Ann wasn't foolish enough to let you type that letter for her. How did you find out what was in it?" His mind raced to think of the possibilities. Had she installed a tiny camera aimed at the principal's computer screen in her absence?

Terry lowered her voice as she attempted to answer without answering. "Let's just say that I found a way to get into her documents' folder."

175

Bishop's response was a mixture of admiration and concern. If Sister Ann ever found out, Terry would lose a job that she really needed as a single mother of two. "Be careful, Terry. Be very careful."

***

When Bishop walked into the restaurant, Orjana greeted him with a smile and motioned for him to walk by several people waiting to be seated. Ron was in a booth facing the entrance. It also afforded him a good view of the dessert case. If he wasn't able to go have lunch at the place he preferred, he was clearly going to make the best of the situation.

"Drinks for you guys?" the Slovenian waitress asked as she placed menus in front of them.

"A Coke for me, please," Ron said as he began reviewing the menu.

"Hot tea for me," Bishop added.

"I'll be bak in a minutes to take your order." She didn't spend time chatting with her repeat customers as the place was really busy at the moment.

Ron quickly made his selection and closed his menu. "Mind if I ask what Terry had to say?"

"Not at all," he said as he checked the menu one more time and then closed it. He gave his friend the gist of the letter that Terry had found. He didn't intend to explain how Terry had found it, and he was relieved that Ron didn't ask. The assistant principal was more focused on the additional duties that Sister Ann was asking of the faculty.

He shrugged his shoulders, and shook his head in disbelief. "I just don't understand what that woman is thinking. Why would she want to antagonize the faculty so soon after her return?"

Before he had a chance to respond, Orjana returned with their drinks. "Vhat can I get for you two?"

Ron gestured for Bishop to go first.

"I'll have the fried haddock sandwich with sweet potato fries."

Orjana was so good at her job that she didn't bother to write anything down. "And for you, Meester Yennings?"

"I'll have the fisherman's platter, please."

She took the menus and disappeared.

Bishop was only mildly surprised by his selection. Teasing his friend, he said, "If that's lunch, I can't imagine what you'll want for dinner."

The conversation returned to Sister Ann's letter.

"Can you imagine how Charlie Mitchell will react to that letter? Sister Ann has already forced him into taking on an extra class without any additional compensation. I'm sure you'll be getting a call from him as soon as he opens his mail on Saturday."

Bishop laughed. "I'll be on my way home by then. If Amy's killer is in custody, I'll be more than happy to deal with Charlie."

"Do you really think you have a chance to get that done?"

"I'm counting on it," he said with no hint of boasting in his tone. "You know, the other thing that bothers me about that letter is the implication that Mayhem and Meany will be ruling the roost once again. I just don't understand why Sister Estelle changed her mind about those two."

Ron's attention quickly pivoted as he spied Orjana heading their way.

She placed the hot platters in front of them. "Pleese enjoy. I will chain you to your seet unteel you eet every bite," she added with a smile.

Hearing her familiar line made them both return her smile. Before she left, Bishop whispered, "I have a favor to ask of you when we're done."

She guessed that the favor was to make sure that she gave the check to him. She could not have imagined what he was about to ask.

***

Bishop didn't resist as Ron offered to pick up the check again. It gave him a chance to talk quietly to Orjana as she ostensibly was clearing the table.

"I think that I'm close to nailing Amy's killer," he started.

"Nailing? What means this?" She gave him a quizzical look. He should have realized that he needed to avoid words that she might misinterpret.

"I'm sorry. It means that I'm close to finding out who killed Amy, but I need your help."

"Me?" Again, she was confused.

"Yes, Orjana."

"She was killed?" she whispered in disbelief.

"Yes, I'm sure that she was. I need you to mention casually to your regular customers that Kelli Dempsey, the secretary at Littleford Realty, overheard her boss talking on the phone with someone a few days before Amy's death. Kelli heard her say that they were going to eliminate that problem once and for all."

She leaned over to whisper in his ear. "Duz dis meen killer is customer?"

He looked at her and nodded. "Whoever took my hat that first day I was here left it at the scene of the crime."

The petite waitress finished clearing the table. She looked extremely worried. "If Kelli knows sometinks, why don't she tell the police?"

"That's a good question. She's very afraid, and if you spread this information around today, we have a good chance of arresting whoever is responsible, and no one will get hurt." He stood up to leave. If he stayed any longer, it might look suspicious, and the person he was hoping to ensnare might actually be in the restaurant at that very moment.

"Will you do this for me, Orjana?"

"Yah. I weel do my best."

"Thank you." As he caught up with Ron, he realized that his plan was far from perfect, but it was better than going home without

179

even trying. He had promised Orjana that no one would be hurt. That, unfortunately, proved to be incorrect.

Chapter Eighteen

If his plan worked, Friday was going to be a red-letter day. Assuming that Officer Minnehan would be able to confirm that Dave Conway was in rehab at the time of the murder, and that Minnehan himself was as eager to uncover the truth about the death of his girlfriend and his unborn child, two of Bishop's original suspects could be eliminated.

Kelli Demspey had readily agreed to participate in his plan to solve the mystery even though it placed her at some risk. With his many years of experience in the classroom, Bishop felt that he was fairly good at reading people. Kelli appeared to have been Amy's friend, and he hadn't picked up any hint of animosity between them that might have led her to lash out. It occurred to him, however, that if Kelli had snuck out of the office that morning and committed the hateful act, she wouldn't hesitate to go along with his plan knowing that it was destined to fail.

Carole Perrault had become the manager of the Belvedere Inn, a position she coveted, as a result of Amy's death. Additionally, he suspected that there was an element of jealousy in that relationship; however, she didn't strike him as the type to resort to a violent confrontation.

Minnehan had questioned Kiki Cavendish, but only because he was there when Bishop discovered the body. Kiki had unsuccessfully asked Amy out, but he wasn't alone in that regard. Amy was very attractive and single. However, Bishop knew that

Kiki was working at Hannaford's at the time the coroner's report indicated that Amy was shoved to her death.

For a brief moment, Bishop considered the possibility that in asking Orjana for her help in setting a trap for the killer, he might have just given the killer a key piece of information. Although Orjana was petite, she might have been able to overpower a startled Amy. And, of course, Orjana could easily have taken Bishop's Tilley hat to put the focus of an investigation on a male suspect. Yet, why would the young Slovenian have wanted to kill the manager of the Belvedere? He had nothing to suggest that this sweet girl was involved.

That left the Martha Littleford – Miriam Littleford Gladstone – Raymond Gladstone troika. There was no doubt in Bishop's mind that they abused their power to enrich themselves. It would probably take months for investigators to unravel the extent of their unethical and illegal dealings. Bishop didn't have months to wait. He decided to force their hand. Making sure that word got back to them that Kelli had some damaging information on them might force them into a mistake.

He wasn't certain what specifically had provoked them to go after Amy. Had she stumbled upon some evidence of wrongdoing? From the phone conversation that he witnessed that first night in Ogunquit, it was clear that they had tangled in the past. Amy wanted to put whatever it was behind her, but Martha might have decided to put Amy behind her for good. She was physically too frail to do the deed herself. Bishop had no doubt of that. She would have hired or ordered someone to follow through.

Her sister, Miriam, had her own reasons for wanting Amy out of the way. She must have been outraged by Amy's audacity to challenge her for her long-held seat on the town board. Having met her only briefly at Bessie's, Bishop had the impression that this woman hadn't walked the Marginal Way in years. She probably didn't even own a pair of walking shoes, and a physical confrontation with the much younger woman would have been out of the question.

That left only one person – Raymond Gladstone. Had he acted on his own? Bishop thought not. As far as he knew, there were no direct tensions between him and Amy. Either Martha or Miriam – or both – had probably asked him to get rid of their problem. In a move orchestrated by Martha, Amy was alone on her jog early that foggy Monday morning. As a longtime member of the Friends of the Marginal Way, Ray probably knew that entire one-and-a-quarter mile stretch better than anyone. He would have known the best places from which to launch his surprise attack on the unsuspecting jogger. Committing the murder there would have seemed to him the perfect location. He knew that he would easily be able to squelch any possible investigation since the news of a murder would do major damage to the local economy which counted so heavily on tourism and positive publicity.

Early the next morning, he would know if his theory was correct.

Walking back to the cottage, he shared his plan with Ron.

"You're taking a big risk, aren't you? I mean, your theory makes sense, but it seems to me, most of the time, someone's motive for murder doesn't make sense."

Bishop appreciated his friend's candid assessment.

"You're correct on both counts," he said. "Murder never makes sense, but I'm trying to look at it from the point of view of the murderer. The problem is that there are so many pieces of the puzzle that are missing. I have to go with what I've got. I know that it's a risk, but at this point, I don't have any other options. If I do nothing before I leave, I know that someone is literally going to get away with murder." Again, he worried that there was something that he had forgotten.

They both looked up as they heard the sounds of an old-fashioned car horn. Some other people on both sides of the street reacted with laughter as they watched the source of the sounds approach. It was Kiki riding that bike and honking that horn. Bishop waved as he passed by. He turned to Ron and laughed. "I'm beginning to understand why Gladstone calls him, 'Cuckoo.'"

***

Ron went into the kitchen to make himself a sandwich. Bishop headed for his favorite spot, the chaise in the front porch. He would have liked to have a cup of green tea with some classical music playing in the background, but the sounds of the water hitting the rocks in the distance and the refreshing sea breeze more than compensated.

He kicked off his shoes, picked up Celia's Thaxter's book, and started turning the pages, stopping to read a few lines here and there. Then he found a line that made him stop. He read it several times. *When in the fresh mornings I go into my garden before anyone is awake, I go for the time being into perfect happiness.* He knew that his experience on the following morning would be nothing like hers. Although he would be up and out before most people were awake, he would not be focused on the natural beauty around him. Above all, he knew that even if his plan worked to perfection, it would bring him no happiness.

Ron came into the porch and sat down on an old wooden recliner, the type whose incline was adjusted by moving a long metal rod along grooves made in the frame. Ron didn't realize that the back of the chair was adjustable until Bishop explained how it worked.

"Not very user friendly, is it?" Ron remarked, noting that there was no way to adjust the chair while actually seated in it.

"Not at all," Bishop laughed, "but I'm sure that it was considered quite an innovation at the time." The veteran teacher remembered that his parents had such a chair in the home where he grew up. Just as the simple way of life that Thaxter had known living on Appledore, one of the small islands a few miles off of the Maine coast, had all but disappeared, he realized that he was living in a world much more complicated than the one in which he had grown up. Was this seventy-one-year-old outsider in over his head in thinking that he could take down one of the wealthiest and most powerful families in Ogunquit and solve a murder that most people believed to be an accident? What if his plan backfired?

Both men sat quietly for several moments. Sensing that his friend was unusually quiet, Ron asked, "Are you okay?"

Jolted from his meanderings, he realized that he was still holding the book and put it on a small table to his right. "Yeah, I'm fine. Just worrying a bit ... Grace always said that she never worried about anything because she knew that I did enough worrying for both of us."

Ron wondered if he and Mary Ellen would be as happy as Mike and Grace must have been. "You must miss her ... especially being in a place that was special to both of you."

"Every day, Ron, every day."

"For what it's worth, I bet that she would be proud of what you're doing."

"Trying to do," he corrected. "Thanks."

***

When Max bounded into the porch, Ron decided that it was time to give him a little exercise. He had found a Frisbee in the back yard that would serve the purpose.

"I don't know that Max will understand the rules of the game," Bishop said as he thought of the dog's abusive previous owner.

"All dogs know how to play Frisbee," Ron announced confidently as he left the room.

Bishop was debating whether or not to watch Max's performance when his cell rang. It was Officer Minnehan.

"I just got off the phone with George Figueroa, and he confirmed that Dave Conway has been at the Maplewood Restorative Center since Saturday. Initially, he wouldn't talk to me. I had to give my contact information to his secretary, and then he called me back. I asked if I could speak with Conway, and he asked me if his patient was under criminal investigation. When I replied that he was not, he refused to let me speak with him directly."

"Why not?" asked a puzzled Bishop who felt that Conway might know something that would be helpful.

"Figueroa said that there were strict rules regarding outside communications during the first week of their treatment program. I couldn't argue with that."

Bishop reluctantly agreed. He thanked Minnehan for his efforts, and then asked him for another favor.

"Depends what it is," he replied bluntly. He then listened as the teacher-turned- detective laid out his plan. When he finished, the officer said nothing.

"Are you still there?"

"Yes, I'm here."

"Well?" Bishop asked impatiently.

"Well what?"

"Are you going to help me?"

Again, his question was met by silence. Then Minnehan asked, "What if something goes wrong?"

"Do you have a better idea?"

Again, his question was met by silence. Then he spoke of another fear. "I could lose my job."

Bishop didn't hesitate to respond. "Seems to me that you've already lost much more than that."

Minnehan exhaled deeply. He knew exactly what Bishop meant.

"All right. I'll be there."

***

Bishop decided to join Ron and Max in their Frisbee toss. As he was putting his shoes on, he realized that there were no sounds coming from the backyard. Before he even opened the screen door, it was obvious that neither man nor dog was there. Had Ron changed his mind and taken Max for a walk? He considered other possibilities. Had Max somehow escaped? Had he headed down to the Marginal Way?

As he went out to investigate, he heard the sounds of a woman's voice coming from the house next door. The properties were separated not only by a split bamboo privacy fence, but also by a row of mature yew trees beyond that. He couldn't quite make out what the woman was saying, but she seemed to be talking to herself rather than having a conversation. With no sign of his friend, his dog, or even the Frisbee that they were supposedly playing with, he called out, "Ron?"

Max barked in recognition of his owner's voice, and the woman stopped her monologue.

"We're over here," Ron shouted. "Back in a minute."

Bishop heard a door close as the neighbor, having no one to talk to, must have retreated inside. A moment later, Ron jogged in from the front entrance, Frisbee in hand, followed closely by an unleashed Max.

"What happened?" Bishop laughed. He had a good idea what the answer would be.

"I flung one to Max, and it just took off. I guess the wind caught it or something." He dropped the Frisbee near the steps leading to the back door. "Come on, Max … let's go in."

While Max went right to his bowl to lap up some water, Ron grabbed a Coke, and popped the lid. As he flopped on the sofa, he said, "When I went to retrieve my errant throw, this lady came out. We had an interesting chat," he added without elaborating.

"Chat?" he snickered. "The only voice I heard was hers."

"Yeah, I didn't have to prime the pump at all. I apologized for my bad throw, picked up the Frisbee, and was about to leave when she made a comment about how much she liked Jack Russell terriers."

"Was that supposed to be a pick up line?" Bishop grinned.

"I sure hope not! She's about sixty years old and not in the best of shape!"

"What's her name?"

189

Ron hesitated for a moment. "She never said. Anyway, I took the opportunity to ask her if she had known Amy Walsh."

"And?" prodded Bishop.

"She did … sort of."

Bishop wished that his friend would just get to the point, if there was one, but he realized that, as with most people, it was best to let them tell the story in their own way. He sat down in a high-backed rocker next to the fireplace and waited for Ron to explain.

"This lady … whatever her name is … is the housekeeper. She doesn't live in that home. She lives in an apartment building on Agamenticus Road."

Bishop looked confused since this appeared to be irrelevant, but he hoped that that would change.

"Guess who lived in the same building?"

The answer seemed fairly obvious at this point. "Amy?"

"Yup, but that's not the best part. This lady said that a moving truck showed up yesterday and cleaned the place out."

Bishop felt a sinking feeling in the pit of his stomach. He had thought that it might be important to check her home for possible clues as to what might have happened in the hours before her death. That opportunity was now lost to him because of his mental lapse. Bishop guessed that the family probably arranged that. Since her death was officially ruled accidental, there would have been no reason for the police to search her place.

"Did you get the impression that this lady knew Amy well? Maybe I should go over and introduce myself." Perhaps he could makc up for his memory lapse by questioning Amy's neighbor. That hope was quickly dashed by Ron's reply.

"No, she admitted that she didn't know her more than to say hello. They both worked a lot of hours, but from her apartment directly below Amy's, she had heard Amy in several heated exchanges with a man in the last couple of weeks."

Bishop's mind raced through the names of men that he had learned during the week had some connection with her. Dave Conway ... Ben Minnehan ... Kiki Cavendish ... Ray Gladstone ... and some other men she may have dated whose names he did not know. "What were they arguing about?"

"She didn't know or she didn't want to say, but she did add that she heard him threaten her once."

"Seems to me it's the former because she didn't seem to be holding anything back," observed Bishop. "Did she ever consider calling the cops?"

"I didn't even have to ask her," he said as he sipped his Coke. "She said there wasn't any point in calling the cops when there was a police car already in front of their building."

"Someone else had called?"

"Not quite. The officer was the man having the argument with Amy."

Bishop felt the blood drain from his face.

"Minnehan?"

"I'm afraid so," Ron said reluctantly.

Bishop put his head in his hands. He had eliminated Minnehan as a suspect in his own mind and was counting on his help in setting the trap. Had he trusted the wrong man? If so, instead of capturing the killer, he might become his next victim.

Chapter Nineteen

Max settled down next to him on the braided rug. Ron received a call from Mary Ellen and went into his bedroom. Those calls usually lasted for some time. It gave Bishop a chance to reflect on the day to come. He realized that his situation was not unlike that of a student facing a major exam, although for Bishop the stakes were much higher. Over the years, he reminded his students that if they had been working hard each day, they should feel confident going in to a test. He discouraged last minute cramming. Students often thought he was kidding when he advised them to get a good night's sleep before the test, have a good breakfast that morning, and actually look forward to the opportunity to demonstrate their skills and their command of the material. Since part of every test involved applying their skills to new material, he always assured them that they would come out of the exam knowing more than when they went in.

He doubted that he would get a good night's sleep before testing his theory regarding Amy's murder. He knew that he wouldn't want a hearty breakfast at 5:00 a.m. Even though he had done all of the preparation that he could possibly do, he felt far from confident. This would not be enjoyable regardless of the outcome. However, he was certain that he would know more at the end of his test than he did at the start. He hoped to learn the identity of the killer.

As he sat there, he drifted back to a time when Amy Walsh was the eighteen-year-old firebrand working on an editorial for *The Beacon*, the school newspaper. She had asked his approval to publish an editorial on the price of a pencil in the bookstore. As Bishop remembered it, Amy documented the concerns of several students. She investigated the facts and determined that the school purchased a gross of pencils (144) for seven cents a piece. However, in the bookstore, one pencil cost twenty-five cents. He remembered her saying that the 300 per cent markup was inconsistent with the school's status as a non-profit organization as well as a Christian institution.

In an attempt to present both sides of the issue, Amy interviewed Sister Pat Meehan. When confronted with the disparity in pricing, Sister's response was something to the effect that "if students came to school unprepared, they should pay a premium" for any items that they needed. She also noted that a sharpened pencil cost an extra five cents. When Amy asked why, Sister Meany replied, "Because a sharpened pencil works better."

Amy's editorial was well written, but Bishop at first hesitated to give his final approval. He knew that nothing would change, except to increase tension between the students and the assistant principal. He asked Amy to sleep on it and get back to him the next day. As Bishop vividly recalled, she did return the next day armed with some new evidence. Apparently, one of the freshman boys, unaware of the controversy and unaware that sharpened pencils cost more, purchased a pencil that he needed to take a math test first period for the requisite twenty-five cents. He asked Sister Pat if she would please sharpen the pencil for him. Without hesitation, in front of other students, she whipped out a large pocketknife and proceeded to hack, chop, and whittle away at that pencil. Chunks of wood and shavings littered the floor as she handed back what she had reduced to a useless stub of a pencil. "Here," she growled as she shoved the pencil back at the startled student. "And clean up this mess on the floor," she barked as she plodded away.

At the time, he must have been teaching William Faulkner's *The Sound and the Fury* because he recalled Amy making the comment that Sister Pat reminded her of Jason, one of the meanest characters in American literature. In one unforgettable scene, Jason has a ticket to a show that he has no intention of using. Luster, the teenage grandson of Dilsey who works for Jason's family, has lost the quarter that he intended to use to gain admission to the show. Rather than giving the boy the ticket, Jason takes a perverse pleasure in burning the ticket in front of the boy, causing him to cry. Dilsey calls Jason a mean man and questions if he is a man at all.

Amy's observation of the similarity between Sister Pat and Jason had some merit, but he certainly could not admit that to her. He said something to the effect that it was inappropriate to make such comments and that people's actions could often be misinterpreted.

Unlike things that Bishop wanted to remember and sometimes couldn't, this memory had come back to him so effortlessly and so vividly. He had given Amy permission to run her editorial, and she never once complained about the flak she took from both Sister Ann and Sister Pat, who whined that she had been misquoted and threatened to have Amy expelled.

As Max shifted his position on the rug, Bishop let that story recede into the background. Perhaps that plucky, brave senior girl years later had stumbled upon a more serious example of financial misconduct, confronted those involved, and in doing so, lost her life. Tomorrow was his chance to even the score.

***

When Ron returned to the living room with a couple of chocolate chip cookies in his hand, Bishop asked, "How's Mary Ellen?"

Ron held up one of the cookies. "Can I get you a few?"

After Bishop waved off the offer, he answered the question. "She's upset that Sister Ann is the principal again. She thought that I deserved it. Of course, she's quite biased in that regard," he admitted.

"Well, I happen to agree with her. Look at what Ann has done in the few days since her return." There was no need to remind Ron that the principal had quickly sought to reestablish her control by undoing some of Ron's decisions.

"Maybe I made a mistake in taking off when I heard that she was coming back. Maybe she wouldn't have acted so boldly." He finished the last cookie and wiped his mouth with a napkin that he then crumpled and launched toward a wastebasket in the kitchen. It fell far short of its intended goal, and Ron jumped up, grabbed the napkin, and released some of his frustration by firing it into the container.

"I must say that I don't agree with you on either count. First, you must realize that nine times out of ten, Ann is going to do what

196

she wants to do regardless. Second, you've been very helpful to me here this week." Bishop hadn't thought to express his appreciation to this point, and this was a perfect chance to do so.

"Me? Helpful? I've haven't done anything."

"You're wrong, my friend. Not only have you helped me fill in some important details, there is something else to remember."

"What's that?" Ron had no idea what Bishop meant.

"We're not leaving until Saturday, and I suspect that your biggest contribution has yet to be made." Ron still had no idea what Bishop meant.

***

Moments later, Bishop's cell rang, and Ron got up to leave, but Bishop indicated that there was no need for privacy. He thought that Terry might be calling to complete her report on the day's activities at Holy Trinity, but it was Sarah Humphries, one of the guidance counselors. She and Terry were best of friends, and it was clear after a few minutes of preliminaries, that she wanted to discuss the events of the week.

"I was so upset when Sister Ann sent the Whites up to my office to make a schedule for Jeff. Ron gave him more than enough chances to turn things around before he showed him the door. I had to be professional and act pleased that that jerk was coming back, and when I found exactly *how* the Whites had convinced Sister to let him return, I was ready to puke."

Bishop decided to let Sarah vent regarding events of which he was already aware. Just at that point, however, she broke the news of the latest developments.

"Not long after the two sisters returned from their lunch with Charlie Mitchell, Sister Ann buzzed me. She told me that she had some second thoughts about giving Charlie that sixth class and that she wanted a few more last minute changes."

Bishop had a feeling that he wasn't going to like where this story was headed.

"Changes?"

"Yeah, Charlie is back to five classes."

"Good for him. I guess the money he spent on a lavish lunch was money well spent. Did they decide to give the new hire Creative Writing? That made the most sense right from the beginning." He was thinking of Cheryl Hearst who had taught that same combination of classes for a couple of years despite her objections.

"Mike, you're forgetting that this is Sister Ann we're talking about. She doesn't always make the decision that makes the most sense, does she?"

"I stand corrected. Who did she stick with that class?"

There was a moment's hesitation. Reluctantly, she simply said, "You, I'm afraid."

Bishop literally jumped out of his chair, startling both Ron and Max. "Me? You've got to be kidding!"

"I tried to talk her out of it, without success. She must have had the phone on speaker because Sister Meany added her two cents.

'He's always talking about how much he loves teaching. He'll probably *love* the idea unless, of course, he decides to finally *retire*.'"

"Good luck with that," he said sarcastically.

Sarah said soberly. "There's more."

Bishop assumed that he knew what was coming next. "I'll have to teach the extra class without pay."

"No, that's not it."

"They're going to *pay* me?" he asked incredulously. He didn't even care about the money, but if they weren't going to pay Charlie, why would they offer to pay him?

"You're not getting extra money because you're not teaching six classes."

At this point, Bishop was totally confused.

"They told me to take your two Advanced Placement 12 classes and combine them into one."

"*That's nuts!*" He shouted at Sarah, but his anger was directed at the bizarre directive given by the principal.

"I know ... I know. Don't shoot the messenger," she replied.

"You're right! Sorry!" After a moment's pause, he spoke more calmly. "If I remember correctly, and that's not a sure thing these days, I had sixteen students in one class and twelve in the other. There's no way I can teach in a seminar style with twenty-eight kids." Bishop found that the seminar style worked best for this advanced class. Since the majority of them would earn college credits for their efforts, he had the students sit in a circle so that each felt a greater responsibility to the group. Bishop, as the discussion leader, sat in the circle with the students.

"Where does she expect me to hold a class that large … out on the football field?"

Sarah started to laugh, but she stopped herself as she realized that Bishop wasn't trying to be funny. She was ready to pull the phone from her ear as she delivered more bad news. "Well … when I redid your schedule, in order to add Creative Writing, I dropped the smaller of the AP classes and tried to fit as many of them into the larger class."

"Go on." He walked into the front porch and sank down on the chaise. The soothing surroundings were a sharp contrast to his inner angst.

"Because of conflicts with other classes, I could only fit three more into that one section," she timidly informed him.

"Let me get this straight. Because Charlie Mitchell wormed his way out of teaching that class by springing for an expensive lunch, nine students are not going to have the chance to earn college credits?" It was a rhetorical question for which Sarah offered no answer.

"I wonder how they plan to explain that to the students and their parents. I know many of those kids are counting on those college credits."

"Sister Pat already thought of that. She suggested that all questions be directed to you."

Bishop didn't issue a threat, but it was a promise. "Whoever asks me will get the truth … the whole truth."

Sarah had known Bishop for years, and she knew that he would not hesitate to do what he said. She also knew that if anyone could change Sister Ann's mind, it was Bishop, and she reminded him of that.

"Don't worry. I have every intention of doing just that when I get back." If he could figure out why Sister Estelle had changed her mind and allowed Sister Ann to return as the principal, he might be able to use that as leverage.

"Do me a favor?"

"Sure."

"Give Sister Pat this message from me: *Nescit cedere.* I wish I could be there to see the befuddled look on her face."

"What does it mean?"

"Rough translation … *He does not know how to give up.*"

"I'll do it … then duck," she said only partly in jest.

It took Bishop a few moments to calm down. When Ron came out to the porch, he was snacking on an ice cream sandwich. Bishop took a few moments to explain the latest developments at school. All Ron could do was shake his head, but it helped Bishop put the sisters' actions into perspective. Compared to the challenge he faced the next morning, their actions seemed trivial. Then he remembered the Latin expression that he wanted Sarah to deliver to Sister Meany. *He does not know how to give up.* Soon, the killer of Amy Walsh would know that to be true as well.

201

Before Ron had a chance to make plans for dinner, Bishop asked him if it would be okay with him if they had a pizza delivered. With so much on his mind, he simply didn't feel up to anything more than that. Ron looked a bit crest fallen as he must have already had some ideas of another place to try, but quickly understood where his friend was coming from. "No problem. Why don't you try to read for a while, and I'll take care of ordering?"

Since he hadn't done much reading during this week, he thought that it was an excellent suggestion. He picked up at the library Donna Leon's *The Girl of His Dreams*, which he had started to read earlier. Commissario Guido Brunetti arrives at the Grand Canal in Venice and sees the dead body of a young girl in the water. The image of her face begins to appear to him in his dreams as he searches for answers regarding her life and death. Only days earlier, he had stared into the face of his beautiful former student. The parallel was too eerie for him to continue reading. There was, however, one glaring difference. Brunetti's experience was fiction; his was all too real.

***

After dinner, Ron decided to watch a movie since the Red Sox had a scheduled off day. Bishop went to bed early, hoping to get some sleep, and hoping not to see Amy in his dreams.

Chapter Twenty

Although he set the alarm on his phone for 4:30 a.m., he needn't have bothered. He was already fully awake. His sleep had been fitful, but dreamless. He shaved and showered and dressed in the clothes that he had selected the night before – a tee shirt, lightweight long pants, a Holy Trinity maroon sweatshirt, and sneakers. He slid open the doors to the deck and felt the chill of the late August morning. He looked towards the sea where lights flickered in the distance. Somewhere in town, Amy's killer was preparing to strike again. His plan was already set in motion. Would it work? By the time the sun had begun its trek across the eastern sky, he would know.

As he made his way downstairs, a confused Max ran in from the porch to greet him. He knelt to pat the dog. "It's too early for you to go out. Go back to sleep," he whispered as he enticed him with a treat to settle down again.

The sounds of footsteps approaching from behind startled him. He quickly turned to see Ron standing there in his bathrobe.

"Sorry if I made you jump," Ron said as he stifled a yawn.

"Sorry for waking you up. I was just on my way out."

"Sure you don't want me to tag along?"

"Yes, I'm sure. We went over this yesterday. I'm putting two people at risk this morning. I'm not going to add another."

"I hear ya. I'll take care of Max, and you take care of business."

Bishop checked his pockets to make sure that he had everything, then headed out.

"Wait!"

Bishop turned around and smiled. Ron was holding the Red Sox cap that he had obviously forgotten again.

***

He walked down Israel Head Road at a brisk pace. There were lights on in some of the homes he passed, but others were still darkened. The quiet of the early morning, especially at the beach, was for Bishop his favorite part of the day. Not today, however. His focus was single-minded as he willed his plan to work.

The first step was to meet Officer Ben Minnehan at 6:00 a.m. where Israel Head Road led into the Marginal Way. A few questions lingered in Bishop's mind as he waited. Which Minnehan would show up? The officer who had initially arrived when Amy's body was discovered or the man with the wraparound sunglasses wearing an American flag tee shirt and cutoff jeans sitting on the short footbridge where the incident occurred? Had he agreed to meet Bishop there in order to help him apprehend the killer, or was he there to silence Bishop who knew too much about his relationship to the victim?

He stood there watching the small waves roll gently towards the shore. As the morning progressed, the wind would pick up, and the waves would be more impressive. The sun's beams made the water gleam so brightly that he had to avoid looking in one place for too long. No one passed him coming from either direction. As he turned to look towards Perkins Cove, someone surprised him from behind.

"Ready?"

Bishop recognized Minnehan's voice. As he turned, he wondered if he would be facing a gun. Instead, Minnehan was smiling. Dressed in a light blue jogging suit, he was ready to help this tenacious older man apprehend the individual who took from him his girlfriend and his unborn child.

"More than ready," he said, relieved that his doubts regarding Minnehan were unfounded. "Just in case, did you bring a gun?"

He patted the left side of his waist.

The two men pressed their way into the thick chaotic growth of Asiatic bittersweet, bayberry, honeysuckle, beach plum, ferns, and viburnum that Bishop assumed provided cover for whomever confronted Amy as she crossed the footbridge. They found a low stone wall that marked a property line, and hid behind it. Their spot provided cover while maintaining their proximity to the action about to unfold.

Kelli promised to text Bishop when she left her house and began her jog. She would be jogging by this spot at approximately 6:30 a.m. just as Amy had done earlier in the week. If Orjana had been successful in spreading the story to her customers, half the town would know that as well. The killer would have a strong reason to fear what she might know and prevent her from talking. Bishop assumed that whoever it was would attack her in the same way that

Amy had been attacked. However, this time, the intended victim would not be alone.

As the minutes passed, Bishop grew increasingly worried. Kelli had yet to indicate that she had begun her run. Considering the potential danger that she faced, had she changed her mind? He couldn't blame her if she had; however, if she had simply informed him of her misgivings, he might have had time to come up with another plan. Perhaps she was already headed their way and had just forgotten to text.

Bishop glanced to his right where Minnehan was on high alert, not only for Kelli as she reached the designated spot, but also for any sound that the killer might make. Was he hiding in the dense jumble of bushes and trees that lined parts of the Marginal Way? Would he follow Kelli as she jogged from north to south? Would he approach from the opposite direction? Might he be using some sort of a disguise so that even if seen, he would not appear to be a threat? Would he have a weapon, or would he simply count on his ability to overpower his victim?

The older man tried to ignore his physical discomfort. When he selected his clothes, he hadn't considered that he would be lying on grass that was heavy with the morning dew. His pants and sweatshirt were beginning to soak through, and his joints were aching, yet he was reluctant to move for fear that their position would be given away. He carefully pulled his cell phone from his pants pocket to check the time. It was 6:17. Why hadn't he heard from her?

He held the phone in his hand as if he could will her message to appear on the screen. Suddenly, he heard movement to his left. Both men turned at the same time to see a squirrel skittering through the underbrush. Bishop displayed a nervous grin, but Minnehan, the seasoned officer, turned his laser focus back on the path where not one person had appeared since their arrival.

Bishop had almost forgotten that his phone was still in his hand as a message flashed on the screen. *Running late ... sorry ... I'm on my way*. It was 6:19.

***

He gave Minnehan a thumbs up and tried to remain calm. He recalled the famous lines in the poem, "To a Mouse", by Robert Burns. *The best laid schemes o' mice an' men/ Gang aft a-gley.* In mere moments, he would know whether his plan had worked or gone awry. As he lay crouched behind the wall, he felt uncomfortably warm, but he couldn't risk the unnecessary movement of taking off his sweatshirt. He glanced again at his phone. 6:23.

Both men tensed as they heard someone approaching the footbridge from the left. By peaking over the wall and peering through the jumble of branches and leaves, they discerned a bare-chested young man running along with the ubiquitous white cords dangling from his ears. Bishop had expected that most joggers were running the level sands of the beach since the tide this morning was going out. However, some runners obviously preferred the challenge of this twisting path with its uneven pavement. The remarkable views afforded along the way made the trek all the more rewarding.

That must have been the way Amy felt. He glanced at his phone again. 6:27.

***

Once Bishop left the cottage, Ron knew that it was pointless to try to go back to bed. Max hadn't settled down either. He was ready for his morning ritual – eating and walking. After Max inhaled his morning allotment of dry food and spent a few minutes searching for the right spot in the back yard, Ron surveyed his own food options that were rapidly dwindling as their stay neared its end. He decided that a cup of hot coffee and a couple of doughnuts from The Village Food Market would be an adequate solution. Just thinking of the aromas of that store made him hungry. Maybe he would also buy some pastries to bring back for later.

Most of the tourists were still in bed, he assumed. There were few cars on the road as Ron and Max walked down to Main Street. These were the commuters, rushing to get to work, for whom tourists such as himself were merely a seasonal inconvenience. A good number of delivery trucks rumbled through town in lower gears, belching exhaust, so accustomed to their route that they probably paid little attention to the venerable buildings of the old town.

Max stopped to sniff at a pot of English ivy and large pink geraniums on the sidewalk in front of a jewelry store that was closed at this hour. Ron gave a slight tug to the leash, encouraging Max to move along. Just at that moment, he heard a woman's scream and a thud … and someone shouting, "Oh, my God!"

He looked up to see a black Prius maneuvering around a double-parked truck and then driving off. The black numbers and letters against the white background of the now-familiar Maine license plate were emblazoned in his memory – 915 HKA. He rushed over to the woman who was now surrounded by several people who witnessed the event as well as the driver of the car behind the Prius who pulled over as soon as he saw what had happened. Someone called 911. Others tried to make the victim as comfortable as possible without moving her as she lay on the ground. Her body was twisted into an awkward position as she landed between parked cars. She wasn't writhing in pain. She wasn't even moving. Ron looked at the woman, but didn't recognize her. He did notice, however, that she was wearing a jogging outfit.

**

Minnehan keep his laser focus on the path as if he were a sharpshooter waiting for his mark to pass in front of the crosshairs of his weapon. Bishop could not resist the urge to check the time. What was keeping Kelli from passing by? Had she stumbled and twisted her ankle? Had she changed her mind and turned around? Had the attacker chosen to make his move from a different spot? Had he been wrong to think that spreading the rumor about Kelli having overheard some potentially damaging information would force the perpetrator into action? He glanced at his phone again. 6:31.

It was at that exact moment that both men heard the sounds of multiple sirens. They appeared to be converging on an area not too far from where they had setup their stakeout. A sickening feeling gripped Bishop. He got to his feet somewhat stiffly.

"You stay here in case Kelli comes by," he told the officer. He didn't give him a chance to argue the point. "I need to see what's going on." He stepped over the wall, fought his way through the bramble, and started walking as fast as he could toward the source of the commotion. He pulled off his sweatshirt and tossed it on the first bench that he passed. If it was still there, when he returned, fine. If not, he didn't really care. Even though he was moving as quickly as he could, he didn't feel that he was making much progress. Over the years, he had walked the Marginal Way many times with Grace, and moving fast was never a priority. This time, it was a necessity.

He held out a slim hope that he would cross paths with Kelli as he made his way back. That hope faded as he entered Shore Road. He could see the flashing red and blue lights of several police cruisers as well as an ambulance as he looked toward Main Street. Vehicles were slowly making their way through the area of the incident with the assistance of a uniformed officer directing traffic. As he got closer, he encountered a number of bystanders who had gathered to watch the proceedings.

He asked a middle-aged man carrying a black briefcase and wearing a light gray business suit, "What happened?"

"Some lady got hit by a car," he replied matter-of-factly. "The driver didn't even stop."

"How bad is it?" he asked as his anxiety level increased exponentially.

The man simply shrugged his shoulders. "The EMTs have been working on her for a few minutes."

Bishop began to gently nudge his way forward. Just as he made it to the epicenter of the activity, the responders lifted the woman, wearing a neck brace and strapped to a stretcher, into the back of the waiting ambulance. His worst fears were realized as he caught a clear glimpse of the woman's face. It was Kelli.

He had been so close. If this accident had not occurred, Amy's killer would have been apprehended in a matter of moments. Now what? He would have to leave Ogunquit tomorrow, and her death would be remembered as a tragic accident, and someone would literally get away with murder.

As the ambulance sped off, the small crowd that had gathered began to disperse. Bishop sat down on a bench outside of the closed bookstore and bent over with his elbows on his knees and his head in his hands. A moment later, he sat upright as if he had been hit by a jolt of electricity. What had he been thinking? This was no time for self-pity. His thoughts rightly turned to Kelli. How badly was she injured? Would she survive? His sense of shame was almost overwhelming. He felt tears well up in his eyes. If he hadn't asked her to play a role in his scheme, she might be getting ready for another day at the office of Littleford Realty. How could he have placed his own frustration at his plan gone awry over the well-being of this courageous woman?

As he thought about Kelli's accident, some new questions came to mind. What if the accident wasn't an accident? What if the driver had targeted Kelli? That would certainly explain why the driver fled the scene. He had been so certain that whoever had killed Amy would use the same method to deal with the threat that Kelli posed. He had been dead wrong.

He called Minnehan to tell him what had happened. There was no longer any need to watch for Kelli on the Marginal Way.

***

Sensing that something was wrong, Minnehan had already abandoned his position and quickly found him sitting on the bench.

"Are you all right?"

Bishop nodded that he was.

"Wait here a minute," Minnehan said. One of his colleagues on the force who had assisted at the scene was getting into his vehicle and about to leave. Bishop watched as Minnehan spoke to the officer. After a brief conversation, he returned.

"Well?" Bishop didn't know what to expect.

"Good news and bad news," he responded bluntly. He went on to explain the bad news first. No one that had been questioned got a look at the driver. Most agreed that the car was either dark blue or black. Their guesses as to the make of the car were all over the place, but most were sure that it was a compact or subcompact. Not much to go on."

"What's the good news?" Bishop asked hopefully.

"The driver left the scene of a personal injury accident. If we find the guy, he's facing a felony. Gladstone won't be able to squash this one." The tone of his voice suggested that he was very pleased with that.

Bishop wondered who had been driving that car. If it were merely an accident, the driver deserved a harsh punishment. However, if Kelli died, it wouldn't be a felony: it would be manslaughter. If Amy's death and this attempt on Kelli's life were connected, finding the driver would solve both crimes. Was it possible that Ray Gladstone himself had been the driver or his wife, Miriam, the elected official that Amy had dared to challenge? What about Miriam's sister, Martha Littleford? If she thought that Kelli knew too much, she might have taken it upon herself to take out her own secretary.

"Hey, I thought you guys were staking out the Marginal Way."

Bishop recognized the voice. He whirled around and put his finger to his lips. There was no need to broadcast that fact in public.

Ron regretted his careless remark and moved on to another topic. "There was a commotion here about ten minutes ago. A woman was struck by a hit-and-run driver. They took her away in an ambulance. Hope she's going to be all right."

"Do you realize who that woman is?" asked Minnehan.

"Nope."

"It's Kelli Dempsey."

Ron's shoulders slumped. "Oh, my! I saw the whole thing unfold."

"You did? What did you see?"

"I was walking down the street when I noticed a black Prius hit that lady and then take off. It all happened in just a few seconds."

"Did one of the officers question you about what you saw?"

"No. I went into the store to pick up a few doughnuts and a coffee for breakfast." Neither man had paid much attention to the fact that Ron was holding one of the doughnuts partially wrapped in white paper. "Oh! I did do one thing right," he said proudly.

"What's that?" asked a skeptical Bishop.

"I got the license plate of that car … 915 HKA," he said as he took another bite of the sugary treat.

Bishop was tempted to berate his friend for not reporting that information to the police immediately. He realized that that would be counterproductive. Instead, he complimented his friend. "Nice work! Now, we're in the game again, and I was right about one thing."

"What's that?" Ron smiled as he finished his doughnut and crumpled the paper.

"The other night I said that you would make a big contribution to this before the week was out. I think you just did."

Chapter Twenty-One

Friday was supposed to be Minnehan's day off, but it turned out to be a busy one. He called in the plate number and rushed to the station in his street clothes. Within moments, all police departments in the area were on the lookout for that car. He feared that the car had been stolen, and that when located, the driver would have abandoned it on some back road. If that happened, the investigation would most likely die a quiet death.

Bishop and Ron Jennings headed back to the cottage. The older man needed a shower and a change of clothes. Kelli was on her way to York General Hospital, and Bishop wanted to get there as soon as possible to check on her condition. Perhaps she had caught a glimpse of the driver and might be able to describe that person to the police. The other reason he wanted to go was that he couldn't think of what else to do. He had foolishly convinced himself that his plan would work, and now that it had not only failed but also caused unintended harm, he was out of ideas. Tomorrow would be Saturday, otherwise known in many beach towns as moving day. Renters had to leave their cottages by noon so that the next vacationers could move in.

Ron understood how his friend was feeling, and nothing he could say was going to help. If the license plate number led to a dead end, he knew that it would be a long ride back to Groveland, especially for Bishop. He offered to accompany him to the hospital, but Bishop asked him if he would stay at the cottage, do some packing and cleaning for their departure in the morning, and of course, take care of Max. Ron had no problem with that. If someone had to clean out the fridge, it might as well be him.

***

Within a half an hour, Bishop came down the stairs for the second time that morning. The expression on his face had changed from one of anticipation to one of worry. He stopped for a moment to grab a doughnut from the bag that Ron brought back along with a cup of tea that he zapped in the microwave.

As he headed out, Ron said, "Give me a call when you find out how she's doing."

"I will," he promised.

Driving south on Route 1, Bishop didn't even bother to turn on WBACH for some classical music. He was too focused on his concern for Kelli's condition and on what he could possibly say to her.

Luckily, he found a parking spot near the entrance to the emergency room. That was about the only luck that he had had all morning. As he left his car, he realized that the car immediately to his left was a black Prius. Bishop's heart raced as he considered the possibility that this was the vehicle that struck Kelli. Could the driver, fearing that she was still alive, have chased the ambulance here to finish the job? If so, he didn't have a moment to waste.

He stumbled as he quickly stepped between his car and the Prius, carefully checking the right side for any signs of damage. There were no dents, no scratches, nothing. The car was absolutely pristine. As he headed toward the hospital, he checked the license

216

plate out of curiosity. It was a green Vermont plate. He smiled inwardly at the idea that this was the car in question, although he knew that stranger things had happened. His thoughts returned to Kelli. As a result of his desperate attempt to find Amy's killer, he feared that Kelli had become his second victim.

On entering the large-than-expected waiting area, he observed several groups of people huddled together, some sitting on the red molded chairs and others standing. An older man, bent over at the waist with his head in his hands, murmured softly as his companion tried to comfort him. A young woman wearing a tank top, denim shorts, and sandals sat close to the door leading into the emergency room itself. She stared at the door as if willing it to open. Perhaps too upset to stand or sit, a few folks paced back and forth. Bishop didn't recognize anyone.

Approaching the desk, a bearded man wearing a white shirt with an open collar greeted Bishop.

"May I help you, sir?"

"Yes. I was hoping that you could give me the latest on the condition of Kelli Dempsey, the woman who was hit by a car in Ogunquit."

Without even glancing at a chart or a computer screen, he said what he probably said many times per day.

"I'm sorry, but HIPAA laws prevent me from providing any information to unauthorized individuals." He looked down at a clipboard in front of him and added, "She's being evaluated right now."

"Thank you." He had no choice but to wait and hope that he would somehow get some news … some good news. A few more people came in. Two heavyset men flanked another man who had obviously injured his right leg. Bishop took a seat in the last row, not wanting to disturb any of the others there who had problems of their own.

He glanced at the large screen television mounted on the wall. A woman was demonstrating how to prepare herb chicken breast tenders. He had no interest in a cooking lesson even at the best of times. He tried to tune out the noise.

From a wooden magazine rack, he picked out a copy of *Yankee*. As a native New Englander, Bishop was familiar with that publication devoted to all things related to those six states. Although it was late August, this particular issue displayed a small snow-covered church in rural Vermont. When he looked at the date on the tattered cover, he realized that his selection was not only out of season; it was published over three years earlier. The hospital perhaps didn't have the funds to provide the latest issues. This copy had been donated by Wayne Phillips, 2 Cranberry Lane, Eliot, ME 03903.

He wondered if Mr. Phillips once sat in this waiting room. Had he been the patient or had he been a loved one? Was he still alive, or had someone donated his old magazines? Although Bishop was doing his best to distract himself, his thoughts kept returning to Kelli and the heavy burden of knowing that he was responsible for putting her in harm's way. Another concern popped into his mind.

What about Orjana? Had she heard what had happened to Kelli? How would she feel, knowing that she was the one to spread the false story that Kelli had overheard sensitive information at her office? What could he possibly say to comfort her?

***

Resigned to a long wait, he began flipping through the pages looking for one of Edie Clark's essays that appeared in each issue. As he did so, the older woman who had been comforting the distraught man approached him.

"Excuse me, sir."

Bishop, somewhat startled, looked up into her reddened eyes. She had used bobby pins to keep her graying hair in place, but some strands had come loose, and she hadn't bothered to fix them. She had on a plain summer dress and leather sandals. He didn't know this person, but she did look familiar to him in a way. Before he could figure it out, she spoke again.

"I overheard you at the desk asking about Kelli Dempsey. You must be a friend of hers. I'm her mother, Lorraine."

Panic gripped him. Had Kelli told her mother what she was really doing that morning? Did she tell her the name of the man who had asked her to risk her life in his attempt to catch Amy's killer? What kind of friend would do that? What could he possibly say to her or to her distraught husband who remained in his seat still bent over in worry? Bishop stood up and gripped her delicate hand in his sweaty palm.

"It's so nice to meet you! My name is Michael Bishop. I rented a cottage through Littleford Realty, and Kelli was so helpful to me." That much was true. He hesitated to add any more details. "I heard about the accident, and I wanted to see if I could find out how she's doing."

She threw her hands up in frustration. "They told us the doctor would be out soon," she said as she checked her watch, "but that was about twenty minutes ago." She gestured toward her husband whose slumped position hadn't changed since Bishop arrived. "That's Kelli's father. He doesn't handle stress very well."

"That's quite understandable."

"We've been praying," she said softly.

"Me too." There was nothing more to say. As Lorraine returned to her husband's side, Bishop sat back down with the unread magazine still in his hands. Kelli's family prayed for her wellbeing; Bishop prayed not only for that, but for forgiveness as well. When he had questioned Martha Littleford regarding her insistence that Kelli be in her office early on the morning of Amy's death, he managed to get Kelli in trouble for giving him that information. Now, his attempt to set a trap for the killer resulted in an attempt on her life.

Each time the door to the treatment area swung open, he hoped that Kelli's doctor was emerging with good news for her family, and each time he was disappointed. As time dragged on, he began to second guess everything that had happened since he discovered Amy's body on the rocks of the Marginal Way. What if

220

her death had really been an accident? Was it possible that she had slipped on the damp and sandy path? What if she had ventured out on the rocks for some reason and then slipped on the jagged stones, landing awkwardly in that crevice?

What if Amy had decided to run for office simply out of a sense of civic duty? Miriam Gladstone might have easily won reelection regardless. What if the Gladstones and Martha Littleford were simply obnoxious monied individuals who believed that the world revolved around them and not the murderers that he imagined them to be? What if Officer Minnchan's boss wasn't on the take, but simply concluded that there was no evidence to justify further investigation?

Amidst all of these doubts, Bishop felt as if his late wife was sitting beside him whispering in his ear, *Trust your instincts.* That had been a running joke between them for years. Whenever he agonized over a decision, Grace would repeat those three words. She would also remind him that that was the same advice that he often gave to his students. Whether the issue was as minor as deciding on the correct answer on the multiple choice section of the Advanced Placement exam, or something as difficult as selecting the "right" college, Bishop believed that if they trusted their instincts, they would never have any regrets.

If it was true then, it was true now. What about the fact that someone had stolen his Tilley hat from the restaurant and planted it at the scene? What about the positioning of the body that suggested that it had been moved? What about the threatening note that Carole had found in Amy's wastebasket? His gut told him that Amy's death was not an accident, and he would continue to believe that even if he left Ogunquit without being able to prove it.

***

The automatic doors leading into the building had opened a number of times bringing in the sick and the injured. Most of the time, he tried not to look. This time was different. A tiny old woman with a bad cough exhaled the last puff of her cigarette as she walked in. Cradling a stack of manila folders in one arm, she walked right up to the desk and demanded in a loud, gravelly voice, "Where's Amy Walsh?" Although Bishop had only met her once, he immediately recognized Martha Littleford.

So did Kelli's parents. Her father sat up straight, looked at the woman at the desk, and began to get up. Her mother held onto his arm, urging him to remain seated. From the way that Kelli's boss treated his daughter, she was obviously not one of his favorite people.

Bishop considered several possibilities for her presence. If she had been part of the plot to run down Kelli, was she here to see the result of that attempt? Was she here to express concern for the woman who had worked for her for the last eight years? Was she merely feigning concern in order to shift any possible involvement in the incident away from herself?

Unsatisfied with the response she received from the bearded man behind the counter to her query, Martha walked away. For a brief moment, Bishop thought that she was going to walk through the door marked *No Admittance* in bold red letters to locate her employee on her own. However, she passed that door as if she planned to take a seat. When she saw Bishop sitting in the back row, she went right up to him.

"What are you doing here?" she snarled.

"I might ask you the same question."

She laughed indignantly. "I'm all alone in that office, and tomorrow is moving day. I wanted to make sure that she was coming in for that." She shuffled the folders from one arm to the other.

This woman had the sensitivity of a ball bearing. "I wouldn't count on that. Her family is waiting to hear from the doctors," as he looked over at the older couple. That look turned out to be a major mistake. Littleford marched right over to them and without even a word of greeting or an expression of sympathy, dumped the folders into Lorraine's arms.

"Would you be a dear and make sure that Kelli gets these? She'll know what to do with them." Before she could turn to leave, Kelli's father stood up. He was taller than Bishop expected, and he towered over the real estate owner.

"Lady, I'll tell you what you can do with those folders." Before Martha could respond, Lorraine shushed her husband and said, "We don't know what condition she's in."

Littleford simply shrugged as if that wasn't her problem, left the folders there, and made her way out of the lobby. Bishop heard Lorraine trying to calm her husband down by reminding him that

Kelli needed that job regardless of how unpleasant that woman could be.

"That's assuming she's okay," he replied ominously as he slouched back down into the chair.

A moment later, a petite woman doctor opened the doors from the treatment area and motioned for Kelli's parents to come in. They held hands as they greeted the doctor and disappeared behind the doors. Soon, the waiting would be over.

Chapter Twenty-Two

The phone rang once, and Minnehan picked up. He listened carefully as he wrote something down on a pad of paper at his desk.

"Good work. Thanks, buddy. I owe you one."

He ripped the sheet from the pad and headed for his car. As he left, he texted Bishop. *Located the owner. On my way there.*

***

Ron Jennings had taken Max for a walk and played Frisbie with him until the dog lost interest. Back in the cottage, Ron tried to keep busy. He surfed the Internet for a while and caught up on the previous night's scores. Mary Ellen had morning classes, so he couldn't call her. He decided to make a quick run to Hannaford's to pick up a few snacks for the ride home the next day.

On the way back, his cell rang. Since he had been expecting a call from Mike, he had his wireless earpiece in place. Hoping for some good news, he pushed the button only to find Terry on the line.

"Are you busy?"

"Not at all. I'm waiting to hear from Mike, so if he calls while we're talking, I'll have to call you back."

"Sure. No problem. What's going on up there?"

Ron proceeded to fill her in on the day's developments. By the time he finished, he had pulled into the driveway of the cottage on Israel Head Road. Michael's Toyota wasn't in the driveway which meant that he was probably still at the hospital.

"I hope that woman is going to be all right."

"Frankly, I'm worried about Michael as well."

"Why? He's okay, isn't he?" she asked nervously.

"He's fine, physically, but if Kelli's injuries are serious, I'm worried about how he's going to cope with that."

"At least you guys are coming home tomorrow, aren't you?"

"Yes, we are, and that's a problem as well. The way it looks now, Michael will be leaving without solving Amy's murder. That isn't going to sit well with him."

"I hear ya. That man is too hard on himself sometimes, but what about that license plate? Maybe that will break the case open."

"Maybe," Jennings replied without much conviction. After a moment's pause, he asked, "Why did you call? Something up?"

"Well," she said excitedly as she switched into storytelling mode, "it's not as important as what's going on in Ogunquit, but it has been an interesting morning around here."

She stopped there to let Ron ponder the possibilities for a moment.

"I assume that the coast is clear."

"Natch. The two head honchos decided to get an early start on the weekend. Sister Pat was getting antsy confined to her scooter, so they took off. You should have seen Ann trying to maneuver her pal into the car. It was hilarious. She had to ask Jack to help hoist her in."

Terry laughed all the way through her play-by-play of the scene. Ron knew that Jack Slater, the school's custodian, would milk that story for weeks to come.

"With those two gone, you should have a delightful afternoon."

"I certainly will, but they managed to drop a few bombshells before they left."

As was habit, she stopped there to allow her listener's imagination to run wild.

"I'm sitting down," he said jokingly. "What are they up to now?"

"For starters, Sister Ann came up to my desk with a copy of the school calendar that you had prepared." Ron braced himself for what might come next. "She told me to make some changes." Again, Terry stopped mid-story for dramatic effect.

"Such as?"

"She insisted that I delete the monthly meetings of the department chairmen."

"Why would she want to do a thing like that?" His tone made clear his confusion.

"That's what I asked, and she proceeded to remind me that my job was to do what I was told, not to ask questions. I swear … I was so peeved I wanted to quit on the spot! This place was so pleasant for a couple of months. Why did Sister Estelle allow her to come back?"

"That's a good question. I know that Michael will be looking for answers when he gets back. He'll be interested to know why those meetings were wiped off of the schedule, too. That gave them a chance to discuss issues and offer some input to the administration whether they wanted it or not. I guess they'll just have to meet on their own now."

"That won't be happening either."

"What do you mean?"

"She not only eliminated the meetings; she eliminated the position of department chairman as well."

"Whaaat?" he shouted.

"She was so smug about it. She bragged, 'They'll be thanking me when they find out. Ten fewer boring meetings for them. One less layer of bureaucracy for everybody else.'"

Ron was incredulous. "Who does she think is going to do all the work that those folks have done without any additional compensation?"

"I guess she didn't think it through."

"My guess is that Sister Pat didn't either."

"Oh, that reminds me. There's one more bit of news."

"What else?" He braced himself for the unknown by dipping into the bag of doughnuts he had picked up at the store. He bit into the double chocolate and walked to the fridge looking for something to drink.

"We have a new student."

As he poured himself a glass of milk, he asked, "That's a good thing, isn't it?"

"Normally, yes, but in this case, it's a definite *no*." Keeping the clincher in her back pocket, she continued, "Her name is Vickie Moreland, and she is a senior transfer from Cincinnati."

Speaking with years of experience, he said optimistically, "Most of the transfers we get work out just fine."

"The operative word there is 'most'; this one is trouble with a capital T."

He was almost finished with that first doughnut and was contemplating a second. Waiting for word from Bishop was stressful, and when he was stressed, he ate … more. "What makes you say that? You haven't even met the girl yet. Did you pick up some information from Sarah about the reason for this girl's transfer?"

"I didn't have to … I met the bitch this morning." That was strong language coming from the usually unflappable secretary.

"What makes you say something like that?"

"The first thing she said when she walked into the office was, 'Jeez, what a dump!' I didn't know if she was talking about me or the school," Terry said laughing. "She's on the chubby side, but she was wearing a low-cut V-neck top and tight jeans. Her hair is medium length, straight, with some streaks of purple. Yuck!"

"Terry, you know as well as I do that first impressions can be misleading."

"Not in this case. This kiddo is a real stuck-up brat. Did I mention her name?"

"Yes, I believe you said 'Vickie Moreland.'"

"Correct! And did I mention that she's related to someone on the staff?"

"Who?" he managed to ask before he held his breath.

"Sister Pat!"

"You've got to be kidding me."

"Nope. Now we have Meany and Mini-Meany!"

After ending the call with Terry, Jennings wondered how much could go so wrong in the few days since the two sisters had returned to Holy Trinity. Then he considered what his friend had been dealing with during the same time frame. It didn't take him long to conclude that he was the lucky one ... by far.

***

Minnehan arrived at 157 Somerset Road and pulled his cruiser into the empty driveway of a modest one-story home about three miles inland. As the garage door lacked windows, he couldn't tell if it was empty or not.

He opened the gate of the chain link fence that surrounded the small front yard, and a dog in the house started barking. From the sounds of the bark, it was a large dog and not very friendly. A woman opened the screen door only a few inches as she looked back at the dog whose bark had become a growl. "Stop it, Rusty! Stop that barking!" Keeping herself between the man at the door and the dog, she said, "You'll have to excuse Rusty. He doesn't like strangers, but he wouldn't hurt anybody. Did Old Lady Wagner across the street call the cops about Rusty again?" She seemed more annoyed than concerned.

"No, ma'am." He showed her his identification. "I'm Officer Minnehan. I'm investigating a hit-and-run accident."

"Hit-and-run? I didn't see or hear anything." The woman, who was wearing a flowered housecoat and pink fuzzy slippers, didn't appear rattled by the officer's presence.

"No, ma'am. The accident took place on Main Street earlier this morning."

"Well, she said dismissively, "as you can see, I haven't been out of the house all morning." She turned back to the dog that had calmed down, for the moment, at least.

"Is your name Constance Pariso?"

"Yes," she said as a puzzled expression crossed her face.

"Do you own a 2015 black Toyota Prius with the license plate 915 – HKA?"

She hesitated before replying, "Yes."

"Ms. Pariso, that car was identified as the vehicle in the hit-and-run accident."

She began to tremble slightly as she shouted, "That's impossible!"

"Is that vehicle in your garage?" he asked soberly as he gestured to the one-car wooden structure beyond his cruiser.

Clearly rattled, she put one hand to her forehead as she held the door tightly with the other. "Well … it was … but it's not there right now."

"I'm afraid I have to ask you if I could come in. I have some more questions for you."

"I'm not in any trouble, am I?" she asked with a sense of panic in her voice.

"No … not yet."

***

Bishop felt that he was in a courtroom waiting for the jury to return a verdict of life or death. The problem was that it wasn't his life or death; it was that of someone whom he had placed in harm's way. Just as he was about to get up to stretch his legs, the Dempseys slowly reentered the lobby area. They were both crying softly. Had they heard the worst possible news that any parent could hear? He wanted to respect their privacy, but he also desperately wanted an answer.

He jumped up, walked up to the older couple, and instinctively wrapped his arms around them. Lorraine whispered in his ear, "She's going to be okay." Their tears had been tears of joy. Bishop felt himself tear up as he absorbed the news. Kelli had been extremely lucky as the car's impact had been minimized as she bounced off of a parked car before landing on the pavement. She had suffered a broken bone in her leg, and numerous abrasions, but no damage to vital organs, and no signs of a concussion.

Mr. Dempsey shook Bishop's hand. "Thanks for being here. You know, it's funny that when I told her that you were here for her, she told me to tell you that she was sorry. She said you'd understand."

"Tell her to concentrate on getting better!" Bishop felt terrible that Kelli thought it necessary to apologize. It was Bishop who needed to apologize for suggesting that she place her life in jeopardy in his unsuccessful attempt to apprehend Amy's killer. He hoped to have a chance to explain that to Kelli before he left Ogunquit.

As her parents made their way to the exit, Bishop noticed that they forgot the stack of folders Martha Littleford left for Kelli. He went over to the chair, picked up the folders, and held them out. "What about these?"

Lorraine said emphatically, "Toss them out for all I care. When we mentioned that Littleford had shown up, not out of concern for our daughter, but to bring her work to do, Kelli managed a little laugh. That woman has always treated Kelli like dirt. Kelli said to tell that monster she's quitting."

"Good for her!" As Bishop walked back to his car, he couldn't help but wonder if that "monster" had something to do with that hit-and-run.

Chapter Twenty-Three

He rolled down the windows to let the accumulated heat escape his car, and he cranked up the air-conditioner. As he left the parking lot, he noticed a black Ogunquit police car pull in. For a moment, he thought Minnehan might be behind the wheel, but a young female officer was driving. The last he heard, Minnehan had located the owner of the car that ran Kelli down and was on his way to follow up. Had he located the vehicle? Was the owner also the driver? Had the driver confessed? Was the driver in custody? Why would another officer from Ogunquit show up at York General? Was it merely a coincidence?

As Bishop made his way north on Route 1, he thought of another possibility. If Kelli had indeed been targeted because of the rumor that he asked Orjana to spread at the restaurant, once it was clear that she was still alive, the perpetrator might consider another attempt. Kelli could still be in danger! Minnehan must have picked up some key information through his questioning of the vehicle's owner ... enough to convince him that the hit-and-run was no accident. Since Bishop didn't believe that Kelli was the victim of an accident any more than he did that Amy's death was accidental, he chastised himself for not thinking of Kelli's continued vulnerability. He was fortunate that Minnehan was on his team.

Suddenly, a blue minivan was in front of him. A surge of adrenaline coursed through his body as he slammed on his brakes, squealed the tires, and swerved slightly before coming to a stop. The van had stopped for a traffic light that he failed to notice.

Thankfully, no harm was done. When the light turned green, he proceeded very cautiously.

"Something's not right!" he said aloud. Over the past couple of years, he noticed that he was becoming increasingly forgetful. It hadn't affected his teaching as far as he could tell, but he had difficulty with details and that was worrisome. In assisting Lieutenant Hodge in several murder investigations back in Groveland, he felt bewildered and confused by conflicting and contradictory theories. There always seemed to be an elusive piece of information that he had gained but was unable to recall. The more he tried to force that knowledge to the surface, the more difficult it became. Perhaps, at seventy-one, he was simply too old to be an amateur sleuth.

"Poppycock!" he said aloud. He had to believe in himself. *Trust your instincts!* He had less than twenty-four hours to put the pieces together. He knew that Grace was with him.

He started to review all that had happened. He was so certain that the attempt on Kelli's life would occur on the Marginal Way in the same spot where Amy had met her fate. Clearly, he had been wrong … but why? What had he missed? Which one of the people that he met during this awful week had he misread?

***

Instead of going straight back to the cottage, he decided to stop in at Bessie's Restaurant. He needed to talk to Orjana if at all possible. He was in a short line of lunchtime customers. When it was his turn, he looked up at the waitress who had come to seat him. Instead of her engaging smile, the Slovenian greeted him with a scowl. "Wan for lunch?" she managed to say as she grabbed a menu and avoided making eye contact with him.

He followed her as she led him to a table for two that had just been cleaned. She dropped the menu in front of him along with silverware wrapped in a napkin. "Sometink to drink?" she asked, barely controlling her emotions.

He whispered, "I know that you are upset. I understand that, but you must realize that I had no intention of hurting Kelli."

"Sometink to drink?" she repeated. "I'm very busy now."

He ordered a lemonade. She swiftly took off before he could say anything else.

It took her longer than normal to return with his drink. Perhaps it was the fact that the place was crowded. More likely, it was that she didn't want to deal with him. He considered the possibility that she might ask one of the other waitresses to take over for her.

She plunked his drink down so hard that a few drops spilled over the top of the glass and onto the table. "Sometink to eat?" she asked coldly.

Even though he had not eaten all morning, he wasn't hungry. When he didn't answer her question right away, she wheeled to leave saying, "I come bak."

"Wait!" he said a bit too loudly as several customers nearby looked over at him. "I just want you to know that I was at the hospital, and Kelli is going to be okay." Some of the anger disappeared from her face. "I also want to tell you how very sorry I am for asking you to do what I did."

"Too late for sorry," she said as she left to attend to another customer.

He drank half of his lemonade. When he realized that Orjana wasn't coming back with his check, he pulled a five-dollar bill out of his wallet and left it under the glass. He noticed that some patrons seated across the aisle from him were leaving. The young man had just signed his check. Bishop asked if he could borrow the pen that he had used.

He wrote on the napkin, *Orjana, I hope that you can forgive me. Michael Bishop.*

As he left the restaurant, he passed the coat rack with its hangers mostly empty. He glanced at the shelf above the rack where someone had left a tightly folded umbrella. He was wearing a Red Sox cap because he left his Tilley there, and someone had taken it. The fact that that Tilley was found at the scene of the crime was part of his reasoning that Amy had been killed and someone had set him up to take the blame. He thought about that hat as he walked to his car. Something bothered him. It suddenly occurred to him that the hat that Minnehan had shown him in the hospital when he was under suspicion didn't have the chin cords. He was sure of that now. The chin straps were essential to prevent the hat from flying off in a strong breeze. Had someone removed them? Why?

Before he got in his car, two young girls walked by passing a phone between them. His phone! He had turned it off in the hospital and had forgotten to turn it back on. The first message he read was from Carole. *Come to the Belvedere as soon as you can. I've found another note.*

***

Bishop drove the short distance to the inn and walked into an empty lobby. Since no one was at the service desk, he rang the bell a bit too forcefully then muffled the sound with his hand. Carole emerged from her office immediately. She was pale and clearly unnerved. Holding a crumpled tissue in one hand, she waved him back into her office, the office that until earlier in the week had belonged to Amy Walsh. Before either one sat down, Bishop saw the note on her desk. All other work had been put to the side.

"May I?" he asked before picking up the note by its top corners.

She slumped into her leather chair, grabbed another tissue from the box on her desk, and nodded her approval.

I'm not taking NO for an answer!

If the paper had been more crumpled, and if he hadn't given the note Amy had received to Minnehan, Bishop would have sworn that this was the same note that Carole had shown him earlier. The message was the same. The paper itself, although it wasn't an ordinary piece of writing paper, was the same. The words were spread on the page with the same type of black marker. The only difference was that there was a straight black line running diagonally along the upper half of the otherwise blank back.

Bishop sat in a straight-backed wooden chair opposite Carole and looked at her. She did not make eye contact with him, but sat quietly with her hands folded around the tissue. Was she playing some sort of game? She claimed to have found the first note in Amy's wastebasket. Why had she even bothered to look there? She claimed that she didn't know who had written the first note, but suggested that it might have been one of Amy's former boyfriends. Specifically, she mentioned David Conway who had also recently been fired by Amy. However, Minnehan verified that Conway was in a rehab facility in Lenox and could not have murdered Amy.

If Carole had written the first note to deflect attention from herself, why would she write a second one identical to the first? Except for Bishop, Minnehan, and the killer, Amy's death was yesterday's news.

"Where did you find this?" he asked sharply.

"I forgot a binder in my car that I needed, so I went out to get it, and it was under my windshield wiper." She was still visibly shaken. "Amy got one of those notes, and she ended up dead," as she shook her head in disbelief. "Who would want to kill me?"

Bishop had no answer. He sat there looking at the note as if somehow the answer would suddenly appear. Unless she was a better actress than Meryl Streep, Bishop was convinced that she was genuinely frightened and her concern justified. But who would want to kill her … and why?

Even if Minnehan's investigation into the hit-and-run resulted in an arrest, one fact was now crystal clear to Bishop. The assault on Kelli that he had instigated by spreading the rumor that she had damaging information on her boss and on the Gladstones had nothing to do with the assault on Amy or the immediate threat to Carole. He had miscalculated badly. He had assumed that Amy's death was motivated by a combination of greed, power, and privilege. With the immediate threat to Carole, he realized that other powerful factors might be in play … love, rejection, and mental instability. One piece of good news was that Kelli was going to recover.

Although Carole might not have realized it at first, the second note was actually good news as well. Had the murderer done nothing after Amy's death, his identity might never have been known. Now, with his threatening warning to Carole, he made himself vulnerable. He had made a mistake. Bishop had one more opportunity to get this right. The killer unwittingly had given Bishop a second chance. He quickly formulated another plan. "I'm going to coordinate this with Officer Minnehan who is a good man. Here's what I think you should do."

***

When Bishop got back to the cottage, the place was empty. He assumed that Ron had taken Max for a walk. He ran upstairs and took a long shower, trying to envision who had written the note that seemed to appear to him like a sunspot whenever he closed his eyes. He grabbed the bag of doughnuts from the counter, a soft drink from the fridge, and settled into what had become his favorite spot, the chaise on the front porch. Instead of enjoying his last day at the beach, he was absorbed in his uncertainty over how events would unfold. When he looked in the bag to make his selection, he noticed that each was wrapped in its own piece of paper. That's when it hit him.

***

A short time later, Ron came in holding a large plastic cup that most likely contained the remnants of one of his favorite drinks, a strawberry shake. His first concern was the latest on Kelli's condition. Bishop told him that she was in surgery to repair a broken leg and that she would make a full recovery. He also mentioned meeting Kelli's parents, and the odd behavior of Martha Littleford at the hospital.

"That woman sounds like a real piece of work." He added with a sly grin, "I know a couple of people like that. I work with them every day."

Bishop caught the reference but didn't comment.

"Have you heard from Minnehan? Have they tracked down that license plate number?" It was his contribution to the case, and he was proud of it.

Checking his phone again, Bishop replied, "He did send me a text that they had identified the owner of the vehicle and that he was on his way to check it out. I haven't heard from him since. Maybe it was a dead end." No sooner had he finished saying that, a call came in from the officer.

"Any luck tracking that plate?"

"I'd call it more than luck. We hit the motherload!" he said enthusiastically.

"What do you mean?"

"That car belongs to one Constance Pariso. When I told her that her vehicle had been involved in a hit-and-run accident, she became very agitated. At first, she refused to tell me who had borrowed her car, but when I suggested that she could be held as an accessory to a possible manslaughter charge if the victim died, she told me that her brother had taken her car early this morning."

Bishop listened carefully, but he was still a bit confused. "What does this have to do with the 'motherload'?"

"Did I mention her brother's name?"

"No. Who is he?"

"Frankie Tataglia."

***

There was nothing wrong with Bishop's memory this time. "Tataglia? That's the guy that Ron met the other morning. He works for the town, but apparently does a lot of work on the side for Gladstone."

"Dirty work is more like it. We picked him up at work. Can you believe he was dumb enough to park that car, damaged front end and all, in the employee lot?"

"Last place I would have looked," Bishop said ironically.

"Once we had him at the station, he started to sing like a bird. He waived his right to a lawyer. Kept saying he wasn't going to take the fall for 'those rich bastards.' He claims it was Old Lady

242

Littleford's idea to take out Kelli, but it was Ray who told him to do it. He insists that he only meant to scare Kelli, not hurt her. He probably didn't mean to push Amy to her death either. I'd say that Littleford and the Gladstones won't be running this town anymore … thanks to you."

"I appreciate the compliment, but I'm afraid you're making one mistake."

"What's that?"

"Tataglia didn't kill Amy Walsh, but I know who did."

Chapter Twenty-Four

Bishop and Ron were up before dawn. They had each packed their cars the night before except for a few essentials. The veteran English teacher opened his bedroom door and stepped out on the rooftop deck, but didn't stay out there long. It was damp and drizzly, disheartening weather if one was beginning an expensive stay at the beach. For him, it was a good sign as it meant that fewer people would venture out on the Marginal Way that morning. Fewer people translated into a better chance for his plan to work.

Although he had not read the book in years, he suddenly thought of Santiago, the old fisherman in Ernest Hemingway's novel, *The Old Man and the Sea*. He had gone fishing farther out to sea than others dared in search of a great marlin. After a long struggle, he succeeded in making the catch. However, before he could bring it to shore, he could not prevent sharks from attacking and essentially destroying the prized marlin. Santiago had lost the battle, but he never accepted defeat.

Whatever transpired in the next moments, Bishop felt a profound sense of loss and suffering … the lives of Amy Walsh and her unborn child … the heartbreak of Ben Minnehan who loved Amy … the pain inflicted upon Kelli Dempsey and her parents … the anguish experienced by Orjana and Carole … and even for the troubled soul who had begun this series of tragic events. Bishop knew that he had to stop this individual from causing any more harm, but he also knew that he would take no pleasure from it.

***

Although the sky lightened, occasional drizzle continued to fall. Bishop's Red Sox cap did little to prevent tiny droplets from accumulating on his glasses. He had found a rain slicker in the trunk of his car, but that didn't prevent him from feeling chilled to the bone. The prospect of what was about to transpire also contributed to his discomfort. A dense fog clung to the coast making it hard for him to see the ocean that he could hear splashing the rocks mere yards from where he was. Instead of hiding behind the stone wall of one of the properties bordering the path as he had done a day earlier, he took cover behind a tall evergreen whose water-laden branches extended to the ground.

7:11 a.m. Carole had texted him when she began her jog. She would arrive at the short wooden bridge at any moment. Other than the sounds of the waves and of the raindrops hitting the ground, it was deathly quiet.

7:13 a.m. Bishop heard the footsteps of a jogger approaching from the left. He steeled himself for a confrontation. The pace of the jogger's steps was that of a tired runner. Perhaps it was that. Perhaps it was her anxiety over what was about to happen. Bishop focused intently on the spot where he expected her to come into view. She was wearing light gray sweatpants and had pulled a pale blue hoodie around the sides of her face to shield herself from the elements as much as possible. As she crossed the bridge, she slowed her pace even more, bracing herself for what was to come.

Nothing happened!

She kept jogging slowly, uncertain of what to do next. Bishop was baffled. Had he miscalculated again? He had been certain that his plan would work. He had everything in place to ensure her safety. What had gone wrong?

7:14 a.m. He heard a jogger approaching from the right. Had Carole turned around? He didn't think so as the cadence of this runner was much brisker. Then he saw a person wearing a maroon jogging suit and a dark headband. He caught a glimpse of the face from the side … it was Orjana!

***

Bishop's heart sank. Was it possible that he had been wrong again? Orjana could easily have taken Bishop's hat in the restaurant. Had Orjana killed Amy … but why? If she was after Carole, the two must have just crossed paths. Had Orjana just pushed her to her death?

Before he could come to grips with that possibility, Carole texted him. He looked at the screen in relief. *Scared to death when I saw that jogger approach. It was Orjana from Bessie's. She just waved. What now?*

It was, indeed, a good question … the *only* question. He had to think quickly before this opportunity slipped away.

Jog back this way, but take your hood off. He tapped in the letters as fast as he could.

You sure?

Yes! He replied. If he was wrong, no harm was done except he would have let the killer escape. *Trust your instincts!* Grace had said. He knew that he was right.

246

***

7:17 a.m. Visibility was still poor, but Carole came into view, this time with the hood flipped back. Just as she reached the wooden bridge, she came to a sudden stop and began to scream. As if a sea monster had emerged from the depths of the ocean, she saw a hand reach up from under the bridge, grabbing a beam for support, and then the other hand.

Carole had stopped screaming and stood there dumbfounded as the figure hoisted himself up. He stood before her with his bedraggled red hair, his bare tattooed arms, and bare feet, wearing only a pair of swimming trunks.

"Kiki!"

As much as Bishop wanted to protect the frightened manager of the Belvedere Inn, he forced himself to remain still. She understood that she needed to draw a confession out of him. He listened intently.

"You didn't call me 'Cuckoo' this time," he said sarcastically.

"Of course not."

"But you and that other one called me that *plenty* of times," he responded angrily.

Carole, perhaps subconsciously, moved away from him a few steps, and he walked forward a few steps as if their moves were a strangely choreographed dance.

"What other girl?" Carole asked innocently. Bishop was proud of her. She was playing her role to perfection … so far.

"You know who I mean," he snapped as he spit with the wind into the sand along the edge of the path. "You ended up with her job, didn't you? I guess I did you a favor." He laughed at the thought. "I guess maybe now you'll be nice to me."

"I try to be nice to everyone," she said as her voice shook. In fact, Bishop noticed that her whole body was shaking, either from the cold wind coming in off of the water, or more likely from her increasing fear of what Kiki might do next.

"That's not true!" He was increasingly agitated, and Bishop wondered how much longer he could wait before acting. "How many times did you just laugh in my face when I asked you out? And Amy did the same thing … even worse … when I asked her out on this very spot just a few weeks ago. I haven't forgotten that."

Carole recalled that moment. Amy had been in a bad mood to begin with, and she was especially harsh with Kiki. She also remembered that, at the time, she thought it was quite funny. She knew that she had to keep him talking until he confessed.

"We were wrong to do that, and I'm sorry, but there was no reason to hurt Amy." She began to look back toward the trees where she knew help waited, but caught herself before Kiki became suspicious. "Why did you have to kill her?"

He flared in anger and took another step closer. *"I didn't!"* He didn't say anything for a moment as if he was reliving the scene. "She tried to push me away, so I pushed back. I guess I pushed too hard because she stumbled backwards, lost her balance, and landed on the rocks." Kiki was staring at the ground. "I scrambled down to see if she was okay, but she must have hit her head. She deserved it, though. She laughed at me."

"Why didn't you call for help?"

He spoke softly now, but Bishop could still hear what he said. "I knew that she was dead … I knew the cops would think I killed her, so I dragged her body to that crevice and took off." He gestured in the direction of the place where Bishop had found her. The tone of his voice suddenly changed as he lunged toward her. *"Now it's your turn!"*

She started to run but slipped on the wet and sandy pavement. He grabbed her from behind and lifted her off of the ground as she struggled to escape. As he neared the rocks, the crack of a rifle pierced the quiet of the morning. Kiki panicked as Carole kicked and dragged her feet … anything to buy a few more seconds. Minnehan and two other officers who had taken up positions to the left and right of Bishop rushed toward him. Bishop, ears ringing from the shot, sprinted onto the path. Ron Jennings, who was also positioned near the footbridge, unleashed Max who had been startled by the gunfire.

The Jack Russell terrier ran so swiftly that he seemed to be flying inches above the ground. His yapping distracted Kiki. As he turned to look at the dog, he loosened his grip on Carole who wrestled herself free. She ran a few steps before collapsing into the arms of one of the officers.

"Max! What are you doing here?" As Kiki knelt down to greet the dog that he had bonded with days earlier, Max emitted a deep growling sound that Bishop had never heard before. When Kiki tried to pat the dog's head, Max responded by nipping his wrist.

Kiki winced in pain as he backed away. "Hey, what did ya do that for?" He sounded like a little boy whose feelings had been hurt as much as his wrist. Bishop pulled Max away as Minnehan and another officer pulled Kiki's arms behind his back and cuffed him. Kiki was dazed and broken.

Drawn by the sound of gunfire, some people began to gather at the scene including Orjana. Quickly realizing what had happened, she went right up to Kiki and began violently kicking him until Ron restrained her.

"Were you going to keel me too?" she screamed.

A part of Minnehan wanted to finish what Orjana had started, and beat this man senseless. This was the man who had taken his girlfriend and his unborn child from him. Instead, he and the other officer maintained a tight grip on Kiki as he read him his rights and arrested him.

Still confused, Kiki looked at Bishop. "Why did Max try to hurt me?"

With Max now sitting calmly by his side, Bishop looked directly into the troubled man's eyes. "Because he didn't want you to hurt Carole … or anyone else … ever again."

Chapter Twenty-Five

Bishop spent a few hours at the police station giving a statement while Ron took Max back to the cottage. Ron did the final cleanup just before noon. He drove his friend's Corolla to the station, walked back to the cottage, picked up Max, and drove the short distance to Littleford Realty. The office was jammed with renters, some just arriving and others on their way home. Without Kelli's help, Mean Martha looked exasperated and overwhelmed, so Ron decided to use the dropbox to the right of the front door to return the key.

Minnehan insisted on walking Bishop out to his car. The young African American woman at the entrance gave Bishop a high five as he walked by.

"It's been quite a week."

Bishop smiled at the understatement.

"Tataglia has given us enough to keep lawyers for Littleford and the Gladstones busy for a long time."

"Couldn't happen to a nicer trio," Bishop said with a smile.

"And you went from suspect to hero in short order."

"I'm not a hero. Just glad that I could help put the perpetrator where he belongs."

"I hope he rots in prison for a long, long time."

"I wouldn't count on that," Bishop cautioned. "Kiki is a sick young man. I would imagine that he would be given a thorough mental evaluation before the district attorney decides on what charges to bring and the defense decides on a plea."

The officer needed time to think that through. "One thing I still don't understand is why he tried to frame you for what happened to Amy."

"I've been giving that some thought myself. I don't think that's what he had in mind. When I met him at Hannaford's on Monday morning, I remember thinking that he looked familiar. I must have caught a glimpse of him at Bessie's Restaurant the night before. That's when he took the Tilley. He probably snatched it impulsively and must have taken the chin cord out because he didn't like it or didn't know how to use it. When he confronted Amy the next morning, the wind must have blown the hat off."

"Makes sense." He paused for a second, then asked, "Do you think it was just a coincidence that Kiki happened to be there when your dog got away from you and started running down the Marginal Way?"

"Not at all. He must have been waiting for someone to discover the body. When Max led me right to the spot, it gave Kiki a chance to prove his own innocence." Bishop laughed a little. "Actually, when you started questioning me because I knew Amy and may have had a reason to kill her, I remember him telling me that he knew I was innocent. How's that for irony?"

Minnehan was still trying to put the pieces together. "I'm assuming that Kiki hid under the wooden bridge that morning just as he did this morning. If he was at Hannaford's that morning, how did he manage that?"

As if he were responding to a student, he replied, "Good question. What do you think?"

He thought for a moment as he rubbed his chin. "The coroner might have been off in his estimate of the time of death. Kiki must have confronted Amy, rushed off to work, then made up some excuse to leave for the rest of the day."

"That makes sense. Don't forget that Kiki had borrowed a car that day so he was able to move around faster than he could on that bike."

Jennings pulled into the parking lot with Max looking out from the window of the passenger door. Bishop and Minnehan shook hands. The officer thanked Bishop again and told him to be sure to look him up the next time he was in town. Bishop agreed to do just that even though he doubted that he would want to return to Ogunquit any time soon.

***

Ron rolled down his window. "Ready to hit the road?"

Bishop walked around to the passenger side and hopped in to the delight of Max and confusion of Ron. "There are a couple of quick stops I want to make first."

"I hope that one of them involves food," he said as he followed his friend's directions.

It was especially busy when they walked into Bessie's Restaurant. Bishop asked the waitress who greeted them if Orjana was working today. Unfortunately, she was not. Instead of taking a table, he asked for a piece of paper and a pen.

253

Dear Orjana, You are a wonderful woman who has much to offer. Thank you for your kindness and for your help during this week.

Sincerely,

Michael Bishop

P.S. I will try to remember to clean my plate at every meal!

***

Ron grumbled each time that they passed a restaurant or fast-food joint. When Bishop spotted Saraci's Floral Shoppe, he asked Ron to stop. He quickly selected two mixed flower arrangements of roses, carnations, lilies, daisies, and baby's breath in a glass vase. The clerk helped him with the addresses that he needed. He sent one to Kelli, recovering at home from her surgery with a message. *You are an incredibly brave person. I will never forget you. Best wishes for a complete recovery. Michael Bishop*

He arranged for the second bouquet to be delivered to the Belvedere Inn on Monday morning. *Carole, You are simply remarkable. Without your help, the mystery would never have been solved. Thank you from the bottom of my heart. All the best, Michael Bishop*

As he got back into the car, Ron asked, "Can we get something to eat now?"

"Wherever you like."

***

Bishop soon found himself seated across from Ron in the Maine Diner in Wells.

"There's one thing I still don't understand. Why didn't Kiki confront Kelli yesterday as you had expected?"

"Why are you reminding me of my failures?" he laughed.

"No, it's not that. I just don't understand why he singled out Amy and then Carole." Ron glanced at his watch, obviously counting the minutes before the arrival of his lunch.

"Well, Amy and Carole had encountered Kiki on the Marginal Way a few weeks back. He had been pestering them, and probably others, to go out with him. Amy told him off in no uncertain terms. He must have been embarrassed and humiliated beyond the breaking point. In his mind, retribution was justified. I'm sure that that incident took place at the same spot where he confronted each of them again. That would have made sense to him."

"Lots of guys get rejected every day, not that I have any personal experiences in that regard, but they don't decide to get 'retribution.'"

"That's true, but this guy is obviously unstable, and he couldn't handle the name-calling, the teasing, and the insults. In situations like that, nobody wins."

"When were you sure it was Kiki?"

"You actually helped me with that."

Ron gave him a dubious look. "I did?"

"Yes, when I took a doughnut from the bag that you had on the counter, I knew."

"A doughnut?"

"Not the doughnut itself, but the paper it was wrapped in jogged my memory. It was the same type of paper that Kiki used to write both of those notes. He would have easily been able to get clean pieces of that paper at Hannaford's."

***

As their desserts arrived, Ron changed the topic of conversation. "With all that's been going on, I haven't had a chance to tell you the latest from Terry." He then proceeded to inform him of Sister Ann's decision not only to eliminate meetings with the department chairmen but also to eliminate the position entirely.

Bishop took another bite of his Boston cream pie. "Doesn't surprise me. No meetings means fewer questions. Without department chairmen, she has more power. The only thing that surprises me is that it took her this long to do it."

Ron went on to explain all of the problems that would inevitably arise. He couldn't understand why Bishop wasn't upset by these developments. Bishop cared too much about the school and the welfare of the students to simply accept these changes. "Aren't you worried?"

"Not really," the veteran responded calmly.

"Why not?"

"Because Trinity is up for reaccreditation this year. She must have forgotten that. She'll reverse course when someone reminds her," he winked. "I also plan on finding out why Sister Estelle allowed Sister Ann to return despite all of her previous transgressions. I think that's well beyond the concept of second chances."

Ron laughed, relieved that Bishop was still in the game. "Oh, there's one more bit of news. Sister Pat's niece is coming in as a senior, and Terry's first impression is that she's going to be a royal pain."

"For you, maybe," he said to the school's disciplinarian.

"Did I mention that she's in your AP class and that Terry has already dubbed her Mini-Meany?"

"Good!" he said loudly as he laughed and wiped his mouth with this napkin. "I love a challenge."

That was just what Ron wanted to hear.

***

It was mid-afternoon when Bishop and Jennings got into their respective cars for the long drive home.

"No sense trying to stay together. I'll have to make a few extra stops for Max."

Ron didn't argue the point. He was looking forward to spending the rest of the weekend with Mary Ellen.

"Safe travels," he said as he lowered the windows of his Sentra. Country music was playing in the background.

"Same to you … and don't forget to slow down going through New Hampshire!"

Ron winced. "Yikes! I had forgotten about that!"

Bishop left the parking lot of the Maine Diner and headed for home. Max had had a good week at the beach, managing to walk on the forbidden Marginal Way twice without incurring a fine for his owner. He seemed ready for the next adventure.

***

Late that night, Bishop walked into his home on Prospect Hill Road. For a moment, he felt an odd sensation as his days on vacation made the familiar seem unfamiliar. Max, having slept most of the way, busily sniffed his way through the house, content to be home.

That night, Bishop slept soundly. He dreamt that he was walking along the Marginal Way with Grace by his side.

***

Several months later, Bishop received a call from Ben Minnehan. Frankie Tataglia agreed to plead guilty to the lesser charge of leaving the scene of a personal injury accident in exchange for his continued cooperation.

Investigators worked to unravel the tangled web of corruption, kickbacks, bribery, and bid rigging that enveloped Wellington Enterprises, Littleford Realty, and the Gladstones.

Martha Littleford sold her business. Miriam Gladstone refused to resign from the town board claiming that she knew nothing of the illegal activities of her sister or her husband. The chief of police resigned under a cloud of suspicion. Ray Gladstone also resigned after an audit of the Friends of the Marginal Way revealed that he had embezzled thousands of dollars.

Kelli Dempsey recovered fully from her injuries. Taking up Amy Walsh's cause, she ran as a write-in candidate against Miriam Gladstone ... and won.

As for Minnehan, he was promoted to detective. He also had begun dating again. He and Carole Perrault were very happy.

I hope that you enjoyed this book. You might also enjoy the other *Michael Bishop Mysteries: Outline for Murder* (2015), *Schooled in Deception* (2016), and *A Question of Judgment* (2017).

I would appreciate it if you would take a moment to leave a review on Amazon.

www.amazon.com/author/anthonypucci

You may also contact me by email.

michaelbishopmysteries@gmail.com

Made in United States
North Haven, CT
04 September 2023

41132314R00157